Nobody's Perfect

ALSO BY MARLEE MATLIN
DEAF CHILD CROSSING

ALSO BY DOUG COONEY
THE BELOVED DEARLY
I KNOW WHO LIKES YOU

Nobody's Perfect

MARLEE MATLIN AND DOUG COONEY

SIMON & SCHUSTER BOOKS FOR YOUNG READERS

New York   London   Toronto   Sydney

SIMON & SCHUSTER BOOKS FOR YOUNG READERS
An imprint of Simon & Schuster Children's Publishing Division
1230 Avenue of the Americas, New York, NY 10020
Copyright © 2006 by Marlee Matlin and Doug Cooney
All rights reserved, including the right of reproduction in whole or in part in any form.
SIMON & SCHUSTER BOOKS FOR YOUNG READERS
and related logo are registered trademarks of Simon & Schuster, Inc.
Also available in a SIMON & SCHUSTER BOOKS FOR YOUNG READERS
hardcover edition.
Designed by Yaffa Jaskoll
The text of this book was set in Bembo.
Manufactured in the United States of America
First Aladdin Paperbacks edition November 2007
4 6 8 10 9 7 5
The Library of Congress has cataloged the hardcover edition as follows:
Matlin, Marlee.
Nobody's perfect / Marlee Matlin and Doug Cooney.—1st ed.
p. cm.
Summary: Megan, a popular and outgoing fourth-grader, is sure that the "perfect"
new girl dislikes her because she is deaf, but persistence and a joint science fair project
help Megan see that the two girls have something in common after all.
[1. Deaf—Fiction. 2. Science projects—Fiction. 3. Schools—Fiction. 4. Autism—Fiction.
5. People with disablities—Fiction.] I. Title: Nobody is perfect. II. Cooney, Doug. III. Title.
PZ7.M4312Nob 2006
[Fic]—dc22   2005016111
ISBN-13: 978-0-689-86986-0 (hc.)
ISBN-10: 0-689-86986-X (hc.)
ISBN-13: 978-1-4169-4976-3 (pbk.)
ISBN-10: 1-4169-4976-3 (pbk.)

Acknowledgments

There are several people I would like to thank. Once again, many thanks go out to my agent, the always patient Alan Nevins. Also, I would like to thank my editor, the wonderful David Gale, and everyone at Simon & Schuster.

In addition there are a few others without whom this book would not have been possible. Thank you to Lin Oliver, Washington Elementary School of Burbank, and Dr. Barbara Firestone of the H.E.L.P. Group—your input was invaluable. To my family and friends who inspired much of the story in the book, thank you. I'd like to also thank Sister Mary Elizabeth; who would have thought that a nice Jewish girl like me would be inspired by a grade school teacher who went on to become a nun? And to Jack Jason, my business partner for the last twenty years, I don't know where my career would be without you. Thank you for all the compassionate work you put out there on my behalf.

Finally, this book would not have been possible without the brilliant writing assistance of my cowriter Doug Cooney. You helped bring Megan to life for more adventures. Thank you.—M. M.

I would like to thank Claire Blanchard of Royal Palm School for her warmth and wisdom, Jack Jason and Lin Oliver for welcoming me to the party, and especially Marlee Matlin for sharing her insights, extending her confidence, and always spreading joy.—D. C.

Contents

Glitter Emergency

"HELP!" MEGAN SCREAMED IN A VOICE SO LOUD she rattled the windows. "I'm having a glitter emergency!"

Megan had meant to sprinkle purple glitter onto her handmade birthday invitations, but only enough to add sparkle to her name. She had folded a piece of purple construction paper and written her name across it in big gooey loops of glue. The plan was to gingerly tap the bottle of glitter so that tiny amounts tumbled onto the glue. But Megan had been in her usual hurry and had forgotten to put the cap back on the bottle. With one quick flick of her hand she had knocked over the bottle, which she'd bought earlier that afternoon at Stratton's craft store. What a mess! Glitter was everywhere.

Leave it to me to buy the giant size, Megan thought as she looked at the mountain of purple glitter covering her desk. Everything was buried in shiny purple flecks, even the notepad where she had written the names of the eleven girls in her fourth-grade class that she was planning to invite to her party.

"Did anyone hear me?" Megan called out again. "I repeat! This is a glitter emergency!"

Megan went to her bedroom door and poked her head out to see if anyone was coming to her rescue, but the upstairs hall was empty. *Where is Mom?* Megan wondered. Her mother was always there to remind Megan to do her homework or pick her soccer shorts up off the floor. Now, in the middle of a glitter disaster, she was nowhere to be found.

Okay, where's Dad? thought Megan. But then she remembered that it was Saturday and he was probably puttering around in the garage. If Megan tried to talk to him now, he'd put her to work washing the car.

Okay, so then, where's Matt? wondered Megan. Her brother was always right in her face when she didn't want to be bugged. Now, in her time of need, where was he?

I'll just have to handle this myself, Megan thought with a sigh of resignation as she walked back to her desk.

Megan Merrill considered herself a very independent person. She could take the bus to school by herself. She could go away to summer camp and not even be homesick. If she could do all that, she could certainly handle a glitter spill, even if it was one for the record books. It seemed to Megan that it was the biggest glitter spill in the history of the human race.

Megan folded a piece of purple construction paper and held it in one hand. She cupped her other hand along the edge of the desk and began to scoop the glitter into a giant pile. Her nose itched but she resisted the urge to scratch. The last thing she needed was purple glitter up her nose—she'd be sneezing sparkles for a week.

After a few more careful strokes Megan had brushed the glitter into a considerable mound. Just as she moved the pile of glitter to the edge of the desk and pushed a chunk of it toward her cupped hand, her older brother, Matt, tapped her on the shoulder.

Megan whirled around. The glitter went flying, scattering all over her rug.

"Whoa!" said Matt. "What's with the fairy dust?"

"Matt! Look what you made me do!" Megan said.

"Me?" Matt said. "You don't need my help making a mess. Check out your room!"

Matt had a point. Clothes were scattered everywhere and there was still leftover wrapping paper and ribbon on the floor from her late-night holiday gift-wrapping session over a week ago.

"At least you could help me clean up this glitter," Megan said.

"I could," Matt answered, "but then I'd be late for practice."

Matt was wearing his baseball jersey and batting glove. Baseball tryouts were coming up, and he was spending a lot of time practicing with the team in the hopes of securing a starting position.

"Besides, I'll get that stuff all over my jersey," Matt continued, "and I am definitely not going to practice wearing glitter. Looking all spangly and shiny is pretty much a baseball no-no." He wagged his finger demonstratively in Megan's face and then headed for the door, but he stopped in his tracks before he got to the hallway. Megan had crawled underneath her desk and was pinching little clumps of glitter from the carpet. Matt walked back toward Megan and knocked his knuckles on the desk to get her attention. He crouched low so that they were eye to eye.

"Tell you what," Matt said, "I'll bring the DustBuster up from downstairs."

Megan smiled. Matt could be a jerk, but most of the time he was an okay brother. "If you do, I'll let you come to my birthday party," she offered.

Matt smirked. "No, thanks. I think I'm seriously busy that day."

"You can't be busy that day," Megan protested. "You don't even know when the party is."

"So when is it?"

"January nineteenth!" Megan exclaimed. She pointed to her desk and the calendar with the big purple circle drawn around that date. "How could you forget my birthday? Mom says I get to have a sleepover slumber party for all eleven girls in my class! Well, twelve if you count me. And I guess you have to count me because *I'm* the birthday girl." She held up one of the finished invitations. It had purple feathers glued around the edge, and it read: MEGAN'S POSITIVELY PURPLE PARTY! The information was all inside, the date, the time, the fact that it was a sleepover—"wear your pajamas!"—and the request that all the guests wear something purple.

Megan had been planning her Positively Purple Party for a year, and she couldn't have been more excited. Everything was going to be purple because purple was her favorite color. She was decorating the house with purple streamers and purple balloons. She and her mom were baking a purple cake decorated with purple frosting. They were making purple punch and purple tea-sandwiches, and the girls were going to give each other manicures with purple nail polish.

"Thanks for the warning," Matt said. "Any night you invite a dozen fourth-grade girls to sleep over at our house is a night I'm definitely going to be busy."

He started to leave again, but Megan hurried from the desk to plant herself between him and the door. She held up her hands and started to gesture in sign language.

"Take that back," she signed. "You're my only brother, and you have to come to my birthday party!"

Megan had been deaf since she was eighteen months old, and everyone in her family could sign as easily as they could talk out loud.

"Okay, okay," Matt signed back. "But I'm not going to wear anything purple!"

"I don't even own anything purple," said Cindy.

"Yes, you do," Megan insisted. "Everybody thinks they don't own anything purple, but they're forgetting that violet and lavender are still purple too."

"Oh!" Cindy exclaimed. "I have some pants that my mom says are lilac."

"That counts as purple," said Megan.

Cindy brightened. She was Megan's best friend, and she certainly didn't want to attend Megan's birthday party without obeying the dress code.

Megan and Cindy were sitting in Megan's dining room on Sunday afternoon. Megan was inviting every girl in her class to her birthday party, which meant she had to prepare a total of eleven invitations. She had carefully stacked the works-in-progress in her bedroom, carried them downstairs, and rearranged them across the dining room table. "I finished writing in glue and sprinkling the glitter," she explained to Cindy. She showed off an example of the front of the invitation with the "Megan" in "Megan's Positively Purple Party!" in spangly letters. "So what we have to do now is glue on the feathers."

Megan raised a plastic bag bulging with tiny purple feathers. It was something she'd found at Stratton's craft store, and it had been too perfect to pass up.

"Purple feathers," said Cindy. "Excellent!"

"I know," Megan agreed. She tugged on the

plastic bag to break the seal, but it was stronger than she anticipated. Megan tugged harder and a small explosion of purple feathers burst from the bag.

Megan and Cindy laughed.

Megan arranged a few feathers as a border on the face of the invitation.

"Oh, that looks good," said Cindy, using her thumb to dig at the glue that had hardened at the top of the glue bottle. "But do we put the glue on the feathers or put the glue on the paper?"

"Better glue the paper," said Megan. "These feathers are too small." She placed one feather in the palm of her hand and pursed her lips to blow it toward Cindy.

"You really don't have to make an invitation for me," said Cindy. "I already know all about the party."

"Of course I do," Megan insisted. "You're my best friend!"

"Best friends forever," said Cindy with a smile.

That was when Matt walked into the dining room and belched loudly to announce his presence.

"Ugh!" Megan shrieked after a few seconds, pinching her nose. She twisted sideways to swat Matt with her arm.

"I didn't think you could hear that," said Cindy.

"Much worse!" cried Megan. "I could *smell* it!"

"Megan has a better sense of smell than an alley cat," Matt explained.

"Hey, Matt," said Cindy, waving with purple-feathered fingers.

"Hey," said Matt, stuffing a banana into his mouth. "Mom's going to be mad when you get glitter all over the dining room," he said, looking over the birthday party invitations on the dining room table.

"You know I can't understand you when you talk with your mouth full," Megan replied.

Matt gestured at the clutter spread across the dinner table and signed, "And you know Mom's gonna be mad."

Megan didn't respond. Instead she reached toward the empty dining room chair beside her and raised the DustBuster. She waved it at

Matt to indicate everything was under control.

Matt shrugged, unimpressed. He gazed over the purple invitations, each one individually written, glued, and glittered. It seemed like a lot of work. "Why don't you just send out an e-mail with the date of the party?"

Cindy sighed impatiently. "Girls appreciate it when you put out an effort," she explained.

Megan looked up from the task of gluing purple feathers, perplexed by whatever Cindy had said to Matt. She elbowed Cindy and shrugged her shoulders to ask, *What's up?* Cindy repeated Matt's question in sign language, and Megan shook her head and rolled her eyes.

"I know," said Cindy. "Can you imagine? All you'd get is an e-mail: 'Come to my party.'"

"Nobody would come," Megan replied.

They finished the invitations and stacked them in a box so that Megan could hand them out the next day, their first day back at school.

"I cannot wait to hand out my invitations!" Megan said with excitement.

"I know!" said Cindy, admiring their work

on the last invitation before handing it to Megan to store in the box. "I'll help you hand them out if you want."

"I'm going to need it!" said Megan. With all the invitations, the box was kind of clumsy. "We'll hand them out at the end of the day so that they don't get crushed or anything."

"And on the first day back at school after winter break," said Cindy, admiring the feathers and glitter. "Just wait!"

"I know!" Megan agreed. "All the girls are going to freak out!"

2

Say Hello

"SAY HELLO TO ALEXIS," MS. ENDEE ANNOUNCED from the front of the classroom.

Megan, Cindy, and all the other fourth graders had barely been able to concentrate on the morning Pledge of Allegiance. "Alexis Powell" was written in blue marker on the whiteboard at the front of Megan's classroom at Wilmot Elementary. A new girl stood beside her name. She clutched a notebook, her head was cocked shyly, and she shifted her weight from side to side. She had shoulder-length blond hair and a smattering of freckles on her cheeks and nose. At Ms. Endee's prompt, Megan and the rest of the class responded with a singsong "Hello, Alexis!" The girl flipped one hand up and offered a slightly embarrassed smile.

As the classroom chattered excitedly about the new classmate, Megan stared curiously at the girl in front of the room. She was slightly taller than the other girls in class—but not because she was wearing shoes that made her look taller. Megan had already checked out the new girl's shoes. Alexis was wearing hot-pink tennis shoes with, Megan was pleased to see, long purple shoelaces tied in a big double knot. She was also wearing a lightweight sweater—extremely cute—embroidered with tiny white flowers.

"I like her sweater," Megan signed to Cindy.

"I knew you would," Cindy signed back. "Me too!"

"It's purple!" signed Megan.

"It's lavender!" Cindy insisted.

"Lavender is purple!" Megan leaned toward Cindy to add in a whisper, "Maybe the new girl is all right."

"She looks nice to me," Cindy enthused.

"Class, class, please!" Ms. Endee said loudly, waving her hands in a downward motion. The class settled down and turned forward to pay attention to their teacher.

Megan turned toward Jann, the young woman on the school staff who served as her sign language interpreter. Whenever Ms. Endee addressed the class, Jann would translate her words into sign language so that Megan could understand them. If Megan had something to say in class, Jann would translate Megan's sign language into spoken words for Ms. Endee. It was a pretty efficient system. On top of that, Jann wore bright red fingernail polish and when she signed, it always reminded Megan of little red butterflies fluttering about. She sat at a small desk alongside the whiteboard so that Megan could read the sign language and observe Ms. Endee in action.

Ms. Endee placed a comforting hand on Alexis, the new girl, and issued a bright friendly smile. "It's not easy transferring to a new school in the middle of the year," the teacher declared, "so I want everyone to put out an extra effort to make Alexis feel welcome." Gazing about the classroom, she spotted an empty desk and continued, "Why don't you sit over there, Alexis?"

Megan and Cindy exchanged a glance. Ms. Endee was pointing to the empty desk by the small classroom sink that they used for arts and crafts projects and science experiments. That particular desk was considered a prime location—and it usually belonged to Tony Rosenblum.

Alexis was already headed for her new seat when Megan shot her hand into the air and loudly declared, "But, Ms. Endee! That desk belongs to Tony Rosenblum!"

Cindy noticed that the new girl twisted slightly to get a closer look at Megan when she passed by their desks. Megan had an unusual way of speaking because of her deafness. It was easy to understand what Megan was saying, but sometimes her voice sounded a little nasal and she wasn't used to articulating her consonants. Everyone in their class at Wilmot was accustomed to the way Megan spoke—but it probably sounded a little funny to newcomers.

"Never mind about Tony Rosenblum, Megan," said Ms. Endee. "Although I'm sure he'll appreciate that you watched out for him."

The students tittered and Megan felt a rush of embarrassment. She sank an inch in her chair. She was only watching out for Ms. Endee; it wasn't like she cared the least bit about Tony Rosenblum.

"I got an e-mail from Tony's parents saying that his family won't return from the holidays for another few days," Ms. Endee explained. "So Tony will have to get used to a new seat when he returns." She smiled at Alexis who was just settling into her new desk, and Alexis returned the smile.

"And we now have thirteen girls in our class," Ms. Endee continued. "We used to have twelve, but Alexis makes thirteen."

Right, thought Megan. *Lucky number thirteen!*

Megan had already done the math. She had eleven birthday invitations to her Positively Purple Party neatly addressed and assembled in a purple box in her purple backpack; she had only counted on a total of twelve girls at her party, including herself. Did she need to make another invitation? Did she have to invite the new girl? What was she going to do about Alexis?

"Thirteen is a baker's dozen," added Ms. Endee. She picked up her trusty blue marker and wrote the words "baker's dozen" on the whiteboard. Snapping the cap back onto the marker, she asked, "Does anybody know why we call thirteen a 'baker's dozen'?"

None of the kids raised a hand. No one had heard the expression before, so nobody had a clue. Ms. Endee often used expressions and vocabulary words that they didn't understand. Then she'd write the word or words on the whiteboard and ask someone to volunteer a definition. No one ever did. Now they waited for Ms. Endee to explain the term herself, as she always did.

Naturally they were surprised when, instead of launching into her own definition, Ms. Endee looked over their heads and said, "Yes, Alexis." She was looking at the new girl.

Everyone in the classroom turned to look at Alexis—and when they did, they saw that the new girl had raised her hand. In fact, it was still raised. "A baker's dozen is when the baker throws an extra cookie or doughnut or muffin into the box in addition to the dozen already inside," said Alexis. "The extra cookie or doughnut or muffin makes thirteen. And that's why thirteen is called a baker's dozen."

"Quite right," said Ms. Endee, obviously pleased.

Megan and Cindy exchanged another look. Megan raised her eyebrows and rounded her mouth to show that she was very impressed. "The new girl is good," she signed to Cindy. Cindy giggled, partly because of the jack-o'-lantern look on Megan's face and partly because she loved the way Megan used sign language as secret code in class.

"And this whole discussion of *bakeries* is such a coincidence," Ms. Endee continued with breezy enthusiasm, "because I have one more surprise for our first day back at school! A little surprise for recess!"

The students shifted excitedly in their seats. Cindy turned toward Megan and signed, "What now?"

Ms. Endee reached behind her desk and then presented a large pink box tied with string and obviously from the bakery. She placed it in the middle of her desk so that the entire class could see it—and naturally, they "oohed" and "aahed." They could smell the freshly baked cookies at the back of the classroom. Megan turned toward Cindy and shook her hands excitedly, which was her own version of sign language for "Hooray."

Ms. Endee leaned over the pink bakery box and announced, "Alexis's mother brought cookies to school with Alexis today. I'm going to distribute them at recess, and I want each and every student to make a point of introducing themselves and thanking Alexis before they eat that cookie."

The class chattered with excitement. Megan twisted in her seat to wave and smile at Alexis. But Alexis was the only student in the classroom who wasn't wild with excitement about the promise of cookies at recess. Alexis sat in her chair with a sweet smile, but she gazed down at the desk as though she didn't want all the attention she was getting.

Megan tilted her head thoughtfully to one side as she considered the new girl. Megan hardly knew Alexis at all except that the girl was smart with cool clothes and that she had a mom who knew about cookies. Megan also liked the fact that the new girl seemed a little shy. It was better than being stuck up. Megan was eager to get to know her better.

When the recess bell finally rang, the students pushed to Ms. Endee's desk to raid the box of cookies. Jann had placed a stack of napkins next to the box and given the stack a twist with her fist so that it spiraled into a fun pattern. "A cookie *and* a napkin," Jann admonished. "A cookie *and* a napkin." By the time Megan and Cindy reached the box, only a few cookies were left.

"I got oatmeal raisin," said Megan, wrinkling her nose. "I hate oatmeal raisin."

"I got peanut butter," said Cindy, wrinkling her nose as well.

"The boys ran off with all the chocolate chips," said Megan with a sniff. She didn't know it for a fact, but it was a fair guess and probably true.

"I'll swap peanut butter for oatmeal," said Cindy, holding out her cookie.

The offer made sense to Megan, and she agreed. "That's why we're best friends," Megan said as she and Cindy swapped cookies.

As they nibbled their cookies, Megan and Cindy headed down the hallway and descended the concrete steps that led to the playground. "What do you think of the new girl?" said Cindy, being careful not to have a mouthful when Megan was reading her lips.

Megan was already searching the playground for Alexis. "We're supposed to say hello and thank her for the cookies," she said.

"What's her name again?" said Cindy.

"Alexis," said Megan. "Alexis Powell." She finger-spelled the letters of Alexis's last name so that Cindy got it right.

"How'd you know how to spell it?" asked Cindy.

"Ms. Endee wrote it on the whiteboard!" signed Megan, with an edge of exasperation. Cindy was her best friend, but at times Megan suspected that Cindy was difficult on purpose.

The two girls scanned the playground for

any sign of Alexis. Suddenly Megan thumped Cindy's shoulder and pointed to the far end of the blacktop. Together the girls looked just in time to see Alexis running at the head of a pack of fifth-grade kids who were playing soccer. Alexis outdistanced the other players with a shuffle step—a quick and efficient one-two-three like she knew exactly what she was doing. She tossed her blond hair over her shoulder and held her ground as two boys advanced on her with the soccer ball. Alexis faked to her left and landed a solid side kick on the soccer ball that sent it scurrying down the length of the field.

Megan and Cindy turned to look at each other, and when they did, their mouths were hanging open, full of cookie.

Megan swallowed before she spoke. "The new girl can play soccer," she said.

"I know," said Cindy, nodding and nibbling.

A couple other girls from class clustered around them as they watched Alexis charge downfield on the offensive toward the fifth-grade boy playing goalie for the other team. Alexis could really run and the girls groaned appreciatively when she elbowed a fifth grader out of her path.

"She's tough," said Megan.

"And she's smart," added Tracy.

"And she's nice," said Cindy, returning to her cookie.

"And I *love* her sweater," said Megan. She glanced at the other girls to make sure they were all in agreement. The girls nodded. They all agreed. Alexis Powell was really something.

Megan took another bite of cookie and turned back toward the field. She didn't want to miss what happened when Alexis reached the goalie.

"She's practically perfect," Megan said thoughtfully. She repeated the new girl's name, practicing the way Ms. Endee had written it on the whiteboard. "Alexis Powell."

The moment Alexis stepped off the soccer field, Megan and the other girls had her surrounded.

"So, Alexis—," one girl began.

"Thanks for the cookies," interjected another.

"Way to kick the ball!" said Cindy.

"Thanks," said Alexis with a shy smile.

Megan burst through their ranks. "And I really like your shoelaces!" she said with a burst of enthusiasm. She pointed at Alexis's purple shoelaces and tugged at her own purple sweatshirt so that Alexis could see that they were both wearing the same color.

All the girls laughed—except for Alexis.

"Um, thanks," said Alexis, somewhat distracted. "Are we back in class yet?"

"Five more minutes!" said Megan, smiling about the whole shoelace thing.

"Great," said Alexis, somewhat cool. She glanced past Megan to the other girls. "So do you bring lunch to this school or is the cafeteria okay?"

"On some days the cafeteria is okay," said Cindy, "but on other days the food is scary."

"On Thursdays they serve sloppy joes," said a girl named Bethany, "and they're always good."

"And Tuesdays is pizza," said a girl named Casey.

"So I should bring my lunch except on Tuesday and Thursday?" Alexis asked.

Megan dove into the conversation. "You could do that except some days the cafeteria serves something really good, so we're in the habit of swapping lunches in case there's something we like," she said. "Like beanie weanie or macaroni and cheese but not the shepherd's pie." Megan made a gagging sound to suggest how disgusted they were by the school version of shepherd's pie.

"Oh, right," Alexis said, but she hadn't been listening to Megan at all. Her nose was slightly scrunched and her brow was furrowed as though she were irritated or annoyed. Megan couldn't be sure, but she sensed that Alexis wasn't the least bit interested in her opinion. Alexis didn't even look at Megan when she spoke; she looked the other way. Megan had the impression that Alexis was avoiding her.

Megan glanced toward Cindy long enough to see Cindy purse her lips into a disapproving prune. "What's up with the new girl?" Cindy signed with a big dose of attitude. Megan quickly turned in the other direction. She didn't want Alexis to think they would sign about her, since she probably didn't know sign language.

"You're probably thirsty," said Megan. "Do you want me to show you the good water fountain?"

"Actually," said Alexis, tossing her blond hair over her shoulder, "I think I know where the water fountain is." With that said, she headed across the school yard toward the good fountain.

Megan, Cindy, and the other girls hustled to keep up with her.

"Where are you from?" asked Cindy.

"Texas," said Alexis.

"Alexis from Texas," said Megan, trying to make a little joke.

"Alexis from Texas!" Cindy repeated, wanting to make sure that Alexis appreciated how funny Megan could be—and that Alexis heard all the words.

Megan nudged Cindy with an elbow. "Hey, that was my joke," she said for only Cindy to hear. "I said it first."

"Yeah, I hear that joke all the time," Alexis replied, not particularly amused but not particularly peeved, either. She had already outdistanced the fourth-grade girls the same way

27

she had outdistanced all the fifth graders on the soccer field. At some point several girls stopped trying to keep up with Alexis and lagged behind. And eventually Cindy and Megan joined them.

"We'll see you back in class!" Megan called after Alexis.

Alexis waved over her shoulder and trotted the last ten feet toward the good fountain—putting a healthy distance between her and the other girls.

"What's up with the new girl?" said Cindy.

"Maybe she's shy," said Megan. "It's okay to be shy."

"Yeah, but why is *she* shy?" asked Brittany. "She's practically perfect."

"She wasn't so shy with Ms. Endee," Cindy observed.

Megan turned toward Cindy and the other girls. "Maybe the new girl doesn't like to make new friends," she signed, slowly and carefully so that they would understand the point.

"Maybe you're right," Cindy agreed, offering a little shrug like maybe it was true and maybe it wasn't.

Megan flapped her wrists dismissively to end all discussion of Alexis. "Stop by my desk when the afternoon bell rings," she said. "I've got something for each of you in my backpack. And spread the word to the other fourth-grade girls in our class too!"

The news that all the fourth-grade girls in Ms. Endee's classroom were included in the surprise made the girls squeal with excitement. "I'll spread the word," said Kaitlyn, a girl in pigtails and new glasses.

"Me too!" said Casey, smiling wide in her brand-new braces. Megan smiled back, but she couldn't help wincing as well. She was creeped out by the sight of braces on teeth. It was one of her pet peeves. And it didn't help that Casey had become the absolute expert on crooked teeth ever since her first appointment at the orthodontist. She talked more now than she ever had before. The very idea of braces was enough to make Megan dance the heebie-jeebies. On top of which, it was practically impossible for Megan to read lips when the person wore braces. She had no use for braces whatsoever.

At that moment Ms. Endee appeared at the far end of the playground. "Heads up!" she cried, signaling the children to form a single-file line and head inside. Jann appeared beside her. "Back to class!" Jann cried, waving her arms overhead and positioning herself on the spot where the students were supposed to get in line.

The girls finished their cookies and wadded their napkins to toss in the garbage on their way back to the building. Cindy lagged behind to trot alongside Megan.

"But Megan," she said, almost breathless with anticipation. "What are you going to do about the birthday party invitations and the new girl? We didn't make an invitation for Alexis Powell."

"When we made the invitations," Megan responded, "we didn't know there was such a thing as Alexis Powell."

"But we do now," Cindy insisted. "What are you going to do?"

"I don't know," said Megan, stalling to think through the problem. She didn't feel right about excluding Alexis since all the other girls in class were invited. Yet she'd only just met Alexis, so it might be weird to have the new girl at the party. And she didn't really want to invite the girl to her birthday party if Alexis was just going to ignore her the whole time.

"So what are you going to do, Megan?" Cindy asked again. They had almost reached the classroom and Cindy assumed that Megan had figured it out.

"I said I don't know!" Megan snapped. She wasn't upset with Cindy, she just wasn't accustomed to the pressure.

Megan still hadn't figured out the problem when the afternoon bell rang and all the girls in class descended on her desk in a flurry of excitement. Megan was relieved that she had Cindy to help her hand out the birthday party invitations. The extra effort she took with the feathers and the glitter paid off big.

"A positively purple party!" Casey cried out joyfully, despite a little difficulty wrapping her lips around the words, because of her brand-new braces.

Megan smiled happily as the girls clustered

around her and eagerly asked questions about her plans for the party.

"Is there going to be purple food?" asked Kaitlyn.

"Wait and see!" teased Megan.

"And purple birthday cake?" asked Tracy Alesia, a girl who was so smart she had been advanced to fourth grade a year early.

"Wait and see!" repeated Megan.

Megan was perfectly happy being the center of attention. Even so, she couldn't help but notice Alexis as she headed out the classroom door. Alexis glanced back at the cluster of girls and waved. "See you girls tomorrow," Alexis said.

"See you tomorrow!" Megan called back. All the girls surrounding Megan fell silent and turned to look toward Alexis at the door. But Alexis was already gone.

"What are you going to do about the new girl?" asked Kaitlyn.

"She doesn't know yet," answered Cindy, coming to Megan's aid.

"I don't know yet," said Megan, who was perfectly capable of answering for herself. "I haven't figured it out yet."

"Well, I know that if I was the new girl in school and all the girls were throwing a huge sleepover and I wasn't invited, I'd feel awful!" insisted Casey.

"Me too," said Tracy.

"Me three!" said Kaitlyn.

Megan sighed. She'd been planning her Positively Purple Party for a solid year, and suddenly it had turned into a huge, unexpected drama over the new girl.

3

The New Girl

"IF WAS THE NEW GIRL," SIGNED MEGAN, "AND all the girls in my new school were going to this big-deal birthday party sleepover and *I* wasn't invited, I'd feel *terrible!*" She punctuated the statement by signing several exclamation points.

"There's your answer," said Megan's mother, Lainee, who was mashing potatoes in a big steel bowl in the kitchen.

"That's not the answer!" said Megan. "That's the problem!"

Lainee set aside the bowl and wiped her

hands off with a kitchen towel. "Well, let me ask you a few questions," she said, pulling up a stool to perch beside Megan at the kitchen counter.

Megan reached for an open bag of tortilla chips. She might as well enjoy a snack while her mother addressed the problem. Lainee grabbed the bag of chips before Megan could reach it. "Not now, you'll spoil your supper," she said, sealing the bag with a big plastic clip and pushing it aside.

"Tell me about the new girl. Do you like her?"

"She's practically perfect," said Megan. "She's smart, she's pretty, and she's amazing with a soccer ball!"

"Who's smart, pretty, and amazing with a soccer ball?" asked Matt. He had been standing at the kitchen door, watching as Megan signed. "Not *you*, right?"

Megan looked at Matt for a second and then stuck out her tongue. Matt stuck out his tongue back at her. They were both too old to be sticking their tongues out, but that didn't matter.

"Enough with the tongues already," said

Lainee. "How would you like it if I stuck my tongue out all the time? I could. I *should*. In front of your teachers. In front of your friends." Lainee stuck her tongue out at Megan and then at Matt.

"Don't do that," Megan and Matt said at the same time.

"So who's the practically perfect girl?" asked Matt.

"It's the new girl at school," said Megan. "Everybody wants to get to know her, but nobody gets the chance!"

"What do you mean?" asked Lainee. "She's in the same classroom, right? Just talk to her."

"I think she's shy," said Megan. "We asked her questions at recess, like 'Where are you from?' 'What do you like?' But she didn't want to talk with us."

"What do you mean 'she didn't want to'?" repeated her mom.

"She just walked away," said Megan. And repeated it in sign. "She just walked away." To make herself perfectly clear, Megan hopped off the kitchen stool, tossed her hair over her shoulder—exactly the way Alexis had done on the playground that afternoon—and walked to the other end of the kitchen.

"Sounds like she's just not *that* into you," said Matt. "She doesn't like you."

"I didn't say that," Megan said defensively.

"You didn't have to," said Matt. "If somebody blows me off like that, I get the message. I can take a hint."

"Matt, you're not being helpful," said Lainee.

"I'm trying to be helpful!" Matt protested.

"Go wash your hands and get ready for supper," said Lainee, shooing Matt from the room with the flick of a kitchen towel.

"I'll never understand girls," Matt mumbled as he headed down the hall.

"What did he say?" Megan signed.

"He said he'll never understand girls," Lainee repeated.

"I just don't get it," said Megan. "We were nice to the new girl. We were nice to Alexis. But she just walked away."

"Was she rude?" her mom asked, opening a drawer to grab silverware for supper.

Megan shook her head. She couldn't say

Alexis was rude. But then again, she couldn't say she wasn't.

"It was just *weird*," said Megan. "Maybe Matt is right—she's doesn't like us." She hesitated slightly before continuing. Then she added, "Besides, I don't think she likes deaf people, anyway."

Lainee had been counting spoons but she stopped. "What makes you think she doesn't like deaf people?" she asked.

"Because she talked to the other girls, but she wouldn't talk to me," said Megan. "She wouldn't even look me in the eye."

"Well. . . ," Lainee began, counting forks and knives until she was ready to give Megan the advice she wanted. "I think. . . ," her mom continued—reaching into the cupboard to search for a serving bowl big enough for the mashed potatoes.

"What do you think?" Megan prompted.

"I think you were right before," said Lainee. "I think this new girl is shy."

"But why should she be shy?" asked Megan. "She's practically perfect!"

"Nobody is perfect," said Lainee.

"This girl is," Megan insisted.

"Who?" said Matt, returning to the kitchen to show off his clean hands. "The new girl who's so smart and pretty and good with the ball?"

"She doesn't like me because I'm deaf," said Megan.

"Don't say that," said Lainee. "I don't like it when you say that."

"But maybe it's true," said Megan.

"Maybe she doesn't like you because you're a *brat*," said Matt.

"I am not a brat!" said Megan. She secretly suspected that she was a brat, but she would never admit it.

"Nobody in this house is a brat and nobody is perfect!" her mother announced. She wiped her hands off on a dish towel and tossed it onto Megan's head. "And there is absolutely no reason in the world why this new girl shouldn't like you."

"But she doesn't, Mom," said Megan, raising her voice. "I can tell! I know when people like me and I know when people don't. I know Matt likes me even though he teases me. And I know this girl doesn't like me because she won't look in my face. And it's because I'm *deaf*."

There was a slightly uncomfortable pause in the kitchen. Matt broke the silence. "I'm out of here," he said, heading for the dining room.

"Set the table," said Lainee, pointing at the silverware on the counter. Matt scooped up the forks, knives, and spoons and headed through the door.

Lainee let another moment pass in the kitchen before she spoke. "Megan," she said.

Megan recognized the look on her mother's face and the hand on her mother's hip. Megan was about to get a lecture. She reached for the bag of tortilla chips so she'd have something to eat during the speech, but her mother swatted her hand aside.

Lainee clasped Megan's chin and turned her head forward so that Megan had no choice but to pay attention to what her mother was about to say.

"Megan," Lainee continued, "not everybody is going to like you and it's not because you're deaf. Not everybody likes *me*. Not everybody likes your *father*. People aren't always compatible, and sometimes you meet new people and you don't get along and not everybody becomes your friend."

"So, great," said Megan. "Then I don't have to invite the new girl to my party."

"Wrong," said her mother. "Yes, you do."

"Mom!" Megan protested, slumping on her stool.

"Maybe you got off on the wrong foot and made the wrong impression, Megan. You have to take a little responsibility for your own actions. She's the new girl and you've got lots of friends. You're in a position to cut her some slack and make a little effort. You don't know whether this girl likes you or not. You only just met her today. You don't even know whether *you* like *her* or not. You said yourself that she was shy."

Megan did think the girl was shy. She didn't understand how a girl could seem so perfect and still be bashful, but Megan wasn't going to deny what she had already told her mom.

"This girl could be your new best friend," said Lainee.

"I don't need a new best friend," said Megan. "I have Cindy."

"A new friend, period," said Lainee. "Everybody needs friends. You need to give people time. Give the new girl a chance. You already told me this girl was perfect."

"*Practically* perfect," Megan said, correcting her mother. "She's not the nicest person in the world."

"Maybe she is and you just don't know it," Lainee continued with conviction. "So your job is to find out. Invite her to your party."

Megan screwed up her lips, not so convinced.

"You can't *not* invite her," Lainee insisted. "What was her name again?"

"Her name is 'the new girl,'" shouted Matt from the other room.

Lainee knew that Megan hadn't heard Matt's joke. She stayed focused on her daughter for an answer.

"Her name is Alexis Powell," said Megan, taking the time to spell the name so that her mom got it right.

"So after dinner," said Lainee, "set aside enough time to do another birthday party invitation to give to Alexis Powell in the morning." With that said, Megan's mom pointed at Megan and the glassware and napkins—that was Megan's cue to help set the table for supper. "Supper's ready," she said. "Let's eat."

David, Megan's father, had to work late that night, so they left a plate in the refrigerator for him to heat up when he got home from the office.

"What's up?" he asked his daughter when he walked into the dining room with his dinner. The table had been cleared except for Megan's homework and the materials for the birthday party invitation. Megan was bent over a piece of purple construction paper, carefully sprinkling glitter over a trail of glue.

"One last invitation to my Positively Purple Party," Megan explained to her dad.

"Who did you forget?" David asked, stabbing his fork into the pot roast.

"I didn't forget anybody. There was a new girl in school today, and Mom says I have to invite her so she doesn't feel left out."

"Well, that stinks," said David, before popping

a chunk of carrot into his mouth. "You don't even know this girl, and you have to invite her to your party?"

Megan cocked her head at her father as though she couldn't believe he'd just said that. *"Dad,"* she said, just a little peevish, "she's the *new girl.* How would you feel if you were the new girl and nobody invited you to the party?"

"Well, first I'd be surprised to be 'the new girl,'" he said. Her father shifted his weight and posed like a cowboy in an old Western movie. "And then I'd be happy to get the invitation."

"Exactly," said Megan, dotting the *i* in the purple-glitter "Alexis."

David reached across the table for the salt and leaned in for a closer look at the birthday party invitation. "Megan's Positively Purple Party," he read aloud.

Megan smiled, and her dad smiled back.

"I'm proud of you, pumpkin," said David, running his fingers gently through her hair. "Inviting the new girl."

"Thanks, Dad," said Megan, trying to focus on the glitter and the trail of glue. She thought about telling her dad what a huge drama it had been trying to decide whether to invite Alexis to her party or not, but then she decided against it. Her dad looked tired and seemed hungry. Megan simply let her dad eat.

Megan tapped her finger in a small dab of glue and reached for the bag of purple feathers. Her dad was working on big forkfuls of broccoli and mashed potatoes. Megan gazed sweetly down the table and waited patiently to see how long it would take him to notice that she had glued a small purple feather to the very tip of her nose.

Megan barely managed to get to school on time the next morning, so there wasn't a chance to hand Alexis her invitation before the first bell rang. She figured she'd hold on to it and surprise Alexis at recess. Even so, Megan couldn't resist telling Cindy what she'd done.

"I made an invitation for the new girl," she signed to Cindy.

"Good," Cindy signed back.

"I had to," Megan signed.

"Of course," Cindy signed back.

Megan smiled. She was feeling just a little proud of herself for doing the right thing. And wouldn't Alexis be surprised when she presented the invitation?

It was all Megan could do to concentrate on Jann's hands as she translated Ms. Endee's news about coming events in the school agenda that month. Jann punctuated her translation with wild gestures and big expressions, trying to match Ms. Endee's enthusiasm.

"The first rounds of the school spelling bee happen later in the week," Ms. Endee announced.

Megan glanced at Tony Rosenblum. Tony had misspelled "occasion" in the final rounds of last year's spelling bee, and it was one of those embarrassing things that he didn't like to be reminded about.

"All the artists in class will want to get going now in order to be prepared for the school art show, set for the spring," Ms. Endee continued. "Paintings, collages, watercolors, clay sculptures. Any and all artists are invited to participate!" She was reading from a green flyer that had been created by the school art teacher.

Normally, Megan might have been excited about the art show but not when she was planning her own birthday party. Megan was busy enough with the decorations, refreshments, the cake—not to mention the gift bags.

"And lastly," Ms. Endee announced, "the school science fair is scheduled for the end of next week. I'll be dividing the class into teams on Thursday so you can get started on those projects."

Megan and Cindy exchanged an excited glance.

Ms. Endee used the science fair as an opportunity to teach the students how to collaborate and work together in teams. Megan and Cindy reached across the aisle to link pinky fingers, certain that Ms. Endee would set them to work together. They had already brainstormed a science experiment involving marigolds.

Megan and Cindy headed for recess as usual—although it took Megan a few moments to retrieve the birthday invitation from her backpack. The rest of the class had already hit the playground. By the time the girls reached the bottom of the stairs, Alexis had sought out a pickup soccer game with the fifth graders.

Megan signaled Cindy that she was going to deliver Alexis's invitation. Cindy nodded. She jerked her thumb toward the girls who were hanging out on the picnic tables so that Megan would know where to find her. Megan smiled and ran across the field with the birthday invitation for Alexis.

"Alexis!" she called out. "Hold up a minute, Alexis!"

Alexis turned around just as Megan caught up with her almost at the center of the field. Alexis turned to Megan with a blank expression on her face. "What?" she asked, with just the slightest trace of annoyance.

"This is for you," said Megan. The manila envelope in her hand contained the birthday invitation.

"What is it?" asked Alexis.

"Open it and see," said Megan.

Alexis opened the envelope and pulled out

the purple birthday invitation. The glitter caught the mid-morning sunlight and the feathers danced in the breeze. Megan laughed.

"It's an invitation to my birthday party," Megan announced as Alexis lifted the cover to read the information inside.

"Oh, I'm sorry," said Alexis, without a moment's hesitation. "I can't go to this."

Megan noticed that Alexis was scrunching her nose the same way she had the day before. "What do you mean?" Megan asked.

"Thanks a lot for the invitation, but I can't go," Alexis repeated. She was forcing the invitation and the envelope back into Megan's hands.

"But what's the matter?" blurted Megan.

"I think I'm busy," said Alexis.

"Oh," Megan replied. "Right. Sure."

"I'm really sorry," Alexis continued. "I just can't go to your party."

"That's okay," said Megan, trying to make the situation less embarrassing.

"Thanks all the same."

"Really," said Megan, with a little edge, "it's all right." At this point she wanted Alexis to drop the subject of her party altogether.

"Okay then," said Alexis. She did the same flip-of-the-hair thing she had done the day before and turned to walk away.

Megan was left in the middle of the soccer field holding the big purple invitation that Alexis had refused. Everyone could see that Alexis hadn't accepted it. Megan was stuck clutching a big glittery, feathery purple invitation, with nowhere to hide!

Megan tried to keep her head high as she walked off the field and back across the playground with the invitation tucked under her arm.

Cindy hopped off the picnic table to intercept Megan. She had watched the whole scene, of course.

"What'd she say?" asked Cindy as soon as Megan was within reach.

"She said, 'No,'" Megan replied bluntly.

"What do you mean, 'No'?" asked Cindy.

"It means 'No,'" said Megan. "What's to explain? I invited her to my party, but she doesn't want to come."

"Forget about her," said Cindy.

"Yeah," Megan agreed. She really didn't want to talk about it anymore. It was spoiling her enthusiasm for her own birthday party. She ditched the invitation in a garbage can to get rid of the unhappy evidence that she had invited Alexis to her party but Alexis refused.

"You didn't want to invite her in the first place," said Cindy, "so it's back to just us. The original girls. Just the way you wanted."

"Yeah, you're right," said Megan. But she couldn't help but feel hurt and confused by the whole thing.

4

A Second Chance

"SATELLITE," SAID CINDY.

"Satellite," Megan repeated. "S-a-t-e-l-l-i-t-e." Megan clutched her hands under the dining room table and quickly spelled through the word with her hand, using the manual alphabet. "Satellite." It looked something like this:

S A T E L L I T E

"Okaaaay," said Cindy, referring to the list of prepared study-words for the class spelling bee. "Marooned." She articulated the word with great emphasis because Megan was reading her lips to understand the word. Sign language didn't necessarily have a specific sign for words like "marooned" or most of the words on the spelling bee list. Cindy could interpret the meaning of marooned by signing "left behind" or "left alone" if she was translating the word in the context of a sentence. But to communicate the word "marooned" by itself, Megan had to read her lips. If Cindy had spelled it out using the manual alphabet, she would have been giving Megan the whole answer.

"Marooned," Megan repeated. "M-a-r-o-o-n-e-d. Marooned." She finished the letters with an edge of impatience.

M A R O O N E D

"These are too easy," she protested. "Give me a tricky word."

Cindy was aware that Megan was under pressure, especially since the class spelling bee was scheduled for the next day. The winner from each classroom won a blue ribbon and went against the winners in the rest of the grade. Then the school winners from each grade went to compete against other schools in the county, then those winners went to compete against other schools in the state— and those winners went to the National Spelling Bee. At some point the blue ribbons turned into trophies and scholarships. "If you win the National Spelling Bee," Ms. Endee had announced, "you can be proud for the rest of your life!" It was a very big deal.

Cindy was also aware that Megan wanted to come home with a ribbon or maybe even a trophy even though she was only an average speller. Megan wasn't anywhere near being the best speller in class. Still, she was determined to give the spelling bee her best shot.

"Here you go," said Cindy, referring to the list. "Cornucopia."

"Cornucopia?" Megan repeated. "I don't even know what that is."

"Yes, you do," said Cindy. "Cornucopia."

"You're making that word up," said Megan.

"That's a nonsense word. That's like 'kabillion.' That word doesn't exist."

"Yes, it does," Cindy insisted. "Cornucopia is that wicker thing, the 'horn of plenty' pilgrims used at Thanksgiving. Remember we studied colonial days at the beginning of the year? You fill it up with little pumpkins and stuff?"

"Oh, yeah, I remember 'cornucopia,'" said Megan, making the shape of the horn with her hands. "But I forget how you spell it."

"You spell it like it sounds," Cindy said before she caught herself. "Oops, sorry, that was stupid of me."

Megan didn't mind. "You spell it like it sounds if you can hear it," she said easily. She grabbed the list of spelling bee words from Cindy and searched for the word until she found the word. "Cornucopia," said Megan. "C-o-r-n-u-c-o-p-i-a." She dropped her hand onto the table and practiced the word once through, using the manual alphabet to let her hand feel the word.

C O R N U C O P I A

"That's no fair," said Cindy, looking down at Megan's hand.

"What's no fair?"

"Spelling the word with your hand while you spell it with your mouth," Cindy replied. "That's cheating."

"How is that cheating?" Megan demanded.

"We can't write the word down when we spell it," said Cindy.

"But I'm not writing," Megan argued. "I'm *spelling*. I'm just spelling with my *hand*."

"I still think that's cheating."

"No, it's *not*," Megan insisted. "Think what you want, but until Ms. Endee tells me that's cheating, that's how I spell." She extended her arm until her hand almost touched Cindy's nose. "So *there*," she said, closing the subject by spelling "there" in Cindy's face.

T H E R E

"There's no point to competing in this year's spelling bee, anyway," Cindy said, pushing Megan's hand away. "You know

Alexis is going to win it. Miss Perfect wins everything."

"That's not true," said Megan. "She doesn't win everything. She's only been here for three days. There hasn't been that much to win."

"Why are you defending her?" asked Cindy. "You're the one she embarrassed on the playground with your birthday invitation."

"I don't want to talk about that," said Megan. "I'm trying to forget it. I don't even want to *think* about that."

Cindy didn't say anything. But she knew Megan, and she was thinking that it would probably take a lot of time to forget about that particular little incident.

"I've decided to give Alexis another second chance," Megan announced.

Cindy could hardly believe her ears. "You've given that girl *seven* 'second chances' already."

"So what?" Megan responded. "She's the new girl!"

"So what? I was the new girl once. Nobody did me any favors!"

"My mom says I should give the new girl as

many second chances as she wants!" Megan argued.

"What!" Cindy shrieked.

The night before, Megan had put a big pout on her face and approached her mother to talk about what had happened in school.

"What's with the long face?" said Lainee, pinching Megan's chin and stroking her cheek.

"I tried to give Alexis a birthday party invitation like you said," Megan explained.

"Yes, and what happened?" Lainee asked.

"She wouldn't even look at it," said Megan.

"What!" said Lainee.

Megan took the opportunity to act out the story of the birthday invitation incident. She recreated the complete blow-by-blow of her exchange with Alexis so that her mother would know exactly what she said and what Alexis said—although, of course, Megan made Alexis seem meaner and much more unreasonable than she had actually been at the time.

Megan's mother listened sympathetically. She stroked Megan's hair and agreed that what had happened was awful. Nobody should have her own birthday party invitation pushed back in her face. By that point Megan had curled up into a ball in the crook of her mother's arm. She felt better getting the story off her chest, but she was still confused about what to make of Alexis.

Megan's mother offered to make Megan hot chocolate with extra minimarshmallows—the way Megan liked it. As Megan's mother dropped the minimarshmallows into the mug, she asked Megan to think about how Alexis must have felt, being the new girl at a new school. She talked about what it was like to be shy. Megan's mother confided that she herself had been rather shy when she was a young girl. Megan had never been shy, so perhaps Megan didn't really understand.

Megan wondered whether she hadn't been right the whole time about the new girl not liking her because she was deaf. But her mom insisted that probably wasn't the case. And even if it were, there was nothing Megan could do to control other people's reactions. Maybe, Lainee suggested, Megan could afford to be the bigger person about what had happened on the playground. After all, Megan had lots of friends at school and the new girl didn't have any. By the time they were sharing the last chunks of marshmallow from the bottom of the mug, Megan had agreed to give Alexis a second chance. As many chances as Alexis wanted.

"But just yesterday you said Alexis was stuck up and conceited!" Cindy was still in a snit.

"I never said that," Megan protested.

"You did so!"

"Okay," Megan said, scanning the list of spelling words. "Maybe I said she was o-b-n-o-x-i-o-u-s." She spelled the word in a flurry. "Obnoxious!"

O B N O X I O U S

Cindy laughed. She grabbed the list and searched for a good word. "An obnoxious . . . barracuda!" Cindy cried. "B-a-r-r-a-c-u-d-a!"

B A R R A C U D A

"She's not an obnoxious barracuda," said Megan. "That doesn't make any sense."

"Well, she's still not very nice," Cindy insisted.

"She's shy, Cindy," said Megan. "And she's new! She doesn't know how to behave."

Cindy sighed. "Megan, you're too accommodating," she said. "A-c-c-o-m-m-o-d-a-t-i-n-g!"

A C C O M M O D A T I N G

Megan didn't tell Cindy, but Megan had already given Alexis another chance. By complete coincidence Megan had been the person behind Alexis when they went through the cafeteria line at lunch that Wednesday afternoon.

Megan had watched as Alexis grabbed a container of chocolate milk from the tub of ice that the cafeteria ladies placed at the far end of the food display. Kids who knew the score at Wilmot Elementary knew that the containers on the top of the ice were never very cold. The containers underneath were always frosty cold. *A new kid wouldn't know that*, Megan thought.

Megan stuck her hand deep into the freezing ice water and retrieved a colder container of chocolate milk. She nudged Alexis's elbow with the ice-cold carton—and Alexis jumped. Megan offered her the milk without saying a word.

"But I already have one," said Alexis, somewhat confused.

"This one is *cold*," said Megan, and she shivered a bit to make sure she was understood.

Alexis smiled the slightest half smile and accepted the chocolate milk. She returned the other container to the top of the tub, but Megan reached for it and forced it underneath the ice.

"So that it's cold for the next kid," Megan explained.

"Thanks," said Alexis.

With that, Alexis turned away and continued down the cafeteria line.

Megan touched Alexis's elbow once more, to encourage her to come sit at a cafeteria table with Cindy and Casey and some of the other girls. But Alexis shook her head, with the same little smile, and headed for a spot on the patio.

Nothing really went wrong, but Megan was still confused. Alexis seemed more than shy. Alexis seemed determined not to make friends.

Megan managed to find another opportunity on Wednesday to give Alexis a second chance when Ms. Endee ran math drills with the students that afternoon. Megan's class was supposed to have learned multiplication tables in the third grade—and most of them had—but Ms. Endee said it was important to cover them again before the class buckled down to the challenge of fractions. The class groaned dramatically at the mention of the word "fractions." Anybody who ever set foot on a school playground knew about the mountains of homework involving fractions. To make math more fun, and to help make fractions easy, Ms. Endee concocted her famous math drills. It was like doing basketball drills only with multiplication tables instead of a basketball.

Here's how the drill went. Each student

wore a paper number on his or her forehead. The students split up and formed one line at the far right and one line at the far left of the classroom. One kid stood at the whiteboard with a marker. When the two students at the head of the lines approached the front of the room, the kid with the marker had only a few seconds to multiply the two numbers and write the answer on the board. The rule was that kids could swap lines or not and even swap places in line so that the order of numbers kept changing as kids advanced to the board. Once the drill was under way the numbers came faster and faster. Jann stood ready with chalk to keep score.

Alexis did really well when she was at the board with the marker. Obviously she'd been pretty good at math before she got to Wilmot.

Megan was advancing through the line, wearing a number seven on her forehead. She lost track of Cindy in the chaotic rush of kids during the drill. As the lines pressed on toward the front of the room, Megan guessed that she was going to be matched up with Casey, who happened to be wearing a number seven as well.

Kids were giggling and getting a little rowdy. As the math drill pressed on, it always threatened to get a little out of control. Ms. Endee clapped her hands and insisted that the kids settle down or she was going to have to cancel the game. Alexis took the few extra moments to frantically write all the multiplication products on the whiteboard.

That was when Megan noticed that Alexis's equations were turning from bright red to a pale thin pink, barely legible at all. The red marker that Alexis had been using was running dry.

Ms. Endee kept a fresh pack of markers in the bottom drawer of her file cabinet. *But a new kid wouldn't know that,* thought Megan.

Risking the wrath of Ms. Endee and the loss of her place in the bustling line of kids pressing toward the board, Megan opened the bottom drawer of Ms. Endee's file cabinet and snagged a fresh blue marker so that she had it ready to hand to Alexis when she and Casey reached the front of the room.

Alexis spotted the blue marker in Megan's hand and quickly snatched it so that she could hurriedly write "7 x 7 = 49" on the board. Maybe it was because of the excitement of the moment, but she didn't even pause to thank Megan. She didn't even offer her usual little smile.

After two more equations Ms. Endee took the blue marker away from Alexis anyway and put Ronnie Jiu at the board. Alexis took her place in the rows of kids, and the game went on. Kids zigzagged across and crisscrossed the room so often that Megan and Alexis never got close to each other.

"I saw what you did," said Cindy after the math drill was over.

"What are you talking about?" asked Megan.

"You gave the new girl a marker during the math drill."

That Cindy, thought Megan. *She notices everything.*

"That was really nice of you," Cindy offered.

"Thanks."

"You said you were going to give her a second chance and you did."

"And it wasn't that hard," Megan observed.

"True," said Cindy with a slight sniff, "but she didn't seem to appreciate it."

"Cindy, you have to give Alexis a second chance too."

"No I don't," said Cindy. "She was mean to my friend."

"I'm the friend she was mean to," said Megan, "and it doesn't matter to me. You and I are going to give her a second chance *together.*"

"How many second chances does that girl get?" Cindy protested.

Megan put her hand on Cindy's shoulder. "Cindy," she said, with a little pat-pat-pat. "You're the only one who's counting."

That afternoon at recess Megan and Cindy got up from their picnic table and headed across the playground toward where Alexis was sitting by herself on a stone ledge.

"Say something nice," said Megan. "And find out if we have anything in common."

"I do like that jacket she's wearing today," said Cindy. It was a blue denim jacket with red stars appliquéd on the sleeves.

"The jacket is fun, but she should wear more purple," said Megan. "She looks good in purple."

"You and purple," muttered Cindy.

They were close enough at this point to look directly at Alexis, and they both smiled as they did. They picked up their pace as though they were headed toward Alexis with a purpose. At that same moment Alexis rose from her perch and headed directly for the bathroom like it was a big emergency.

Megan and Cindy stopped in their tracks. They exchanged a glance.

"What was that about?" asked Cindy. "I'm not going to chase her into the bathroom!"

"Maybe she had to go," said Megan.

"Maybe," said Cindy. "But at some point— you know—I get the hint."

"What hint?" asked Megan.

"Maybe," said Cindy, "she just doesn't like us."

It didn't help matters when Ms. Endee conducted the classroom spelling bee on Thursday. Ms. Endee stood at a podium, reciting the contest words in a very official manner. Jann stood beside the teacher, signing the general meaning of Ms. Endee's remarks but not the specific contest words. The situation was a little tricky. Megan had to rely on her ability to read lips to get the contest words. Otherwise Jann would have been spelling the words for her in advance using the manual alphabet and there would have been no contest for Megan at all.

Cindy had to be dropped in the opening rounds when she stumbled over the word "referendum." But Megan surprised herself. She made it all the way to the classroom quarter-finals. In fact, it was down to Casey, Ronnie Jiu, Megan—and Alexis.

Casey correctly spelled "privilege."

Ronnie Jiu correctly spelled "establishment."

Megan grinned. "Privilege" and "establishment" were easy to spell, so Megan figured Ms. Endee was giving them an easy round.

Ms. Endee turned toward Megan and said, "Tandoori."

"Tandoori?" said Megan. "I don't even know what it is!"

"You may ask for a definition," Ms. Endee suggested. Jann signed the suggestion.

"May I have a definition?" said Megan.

"Tandoori is an Indian dish," said Ms. Endee. Megan waited for Jann's sign language translation. Jann thought for a moment, then she signed the phrase, "*It* is a dish from India," and she spelled the word "India" slowly and carefully.

I N D I A

Oh, great, thought Megan.

"Would you use it in a sentence, please?" said Megan.

"I'll have the tandoori chicken, please," said Ms. Endee, and the whole class laughed. Jann signed the sound of laughter—and then she signed the phrase as, "I'll have the—spelling word—chicken, please."

Megan took a stab at a spelling, but tried "t-a-n-d-u-r-i-e." Megan's only chance at remaining in the spelling bee was if Alexis misspelled her word. Then they'd be in a sudden heat, and Megan would stand another chance at the semifinals.

"All right, Alexis," said Ms. Endee. "If you spell this word correctly, you'll go on to our semifinals. If you miss, then you and Megan will be in a sudden heat."

The class cooed with excitement.

"Are you ready, Alexis?" asked Ms. Endee, shamelessly building the suspense.

"I'm ready," said Alexis.

Megan crossed her fingers. *Make it a tough word*, she thought. *Make it something impossibly difficult.*

"Alexis," said Ms. Endee, with a dramatic pause, "would you please spell the word 'cornucopia'?"

Alexis smiled.

5

Nowhere to Hide

"NOT FAIR," SAID CINDY. "IT'S NOT FAIR! TO-TALLY not fair!"

"It was the luck of the draw," said Megan. "Fair is fair."

"But cornucopia was *your* word!"

"It's everybody's word," said Megan. "Nobody owns it."

"What is up with you?" asked Cindy. "I think you're *glad* Alexis won the spelling bee."

"She didn't win," Megan responded. "She beat *me*, true. But Ronnie Jiu won."

"Only because Alexis forgot about '*i* before *e* except after *c*,'" said Cindy.

The final word had been "perceive," a total softball as far as Megan was concerned. But Alexis had blown it. She was headed in the right direction, but then she took a wrong turn after the *c*, and, well, the rest is spelling bee history. Ronnie Jiu had stepped forward and spelled "perceive" as easily as if he'd been spelling his own name.

Ms. Endee said, "I'm sorry, Alexis."

Ronnie Jiu smirked with confidence. Alexis simply shrugged.

"It was a pretty stupid mistake, if you think about it," Megan observed. "*I* before *e*! Who doesn't know '*I* before *e* except after *c*'!"

"True," said Cindy. "Maybe Alexis is human after all."

"Or maybe she didn't want to win," said Megan.

Both girls fell quiet. It was a thought that hadn't occurred to them before. Could Alexis have deliberately thrown the final round of the spelling bee to avoid drawing attention to herself? Could anybody be that shy?

"Nah, it couldn't be," said Cindy. "Not where there are blue ribbons and trophies involved."

"You never know," said Megan.

Everyone in the fourth grade was allowed to pick his or her own book to read and write a report on.

Megan enjoyed reading. In fact, Megan read so many books that she could have written a report on a book she'd already read. But she enjoyed books so much that she wanted to read something new.

Megan was the kind of reader who relied on other readers' recommendations. She was searching through the library for a copy of *Island of the Blue Dolphins* that her mother had recommended. When Megan happened to mention her mother's recommendation, Jann got all excited. "That's one of my favorite books," Jann said.

"Me too," Ms. Endee agreed.

Somebody named Scott O'Dell wrote it, but when Megan reached the *O* section of the shelves of fiction, she was surprised to find

Alexis standing in the stacks holding a copy of *Island of the Blue Dolphins*.

"Are you going to read that?" Megan asked.

"I'm sorry?" Alexis whispered. It wasn't the whisper that annoyed Megan. She knew that people were supposed to whisper in libraries. It was just that something about the effort to whisper made it seem like Alexis didn't want Megan to be talking to her.

"That's my book," said Megan, pointing to the copy of *Island of the Blue Dolphins.* "I came to the library to read that book."

"What if I was going to read it?" Alexis asked, holding her ground.

"I'm reading it for the report in class," said Megan, asserting herself. She had noticed that Alexis was scrunching her nose again.

"So take it," said Alexis. "I've already read it. I was just flipping through the pages to reread my favorite parts."

Megan felt a little ashamed that she had been so gruff about the book and that Alexis had handed it over so easily. She turned the book over in her hands. It looked pretty well worn. "Must be good, huh?" Megan asked, running her hands over the threadbare cover. "You already read it?"

"Twice," said Alexis. "So I really don't need to read it again." She turned her attention back to the shelves, browsing over titles.

Megan was ready to take the book and head for the checkout desk but then she thought of her mother and how shy her mother had been. Megan also remembered how her mother had said that she wished that other girls had been nicer to her when she was a girl. What was one more second chance?

Megan hesitated, and then spoke to Alexis again. "Maybe you could recommend other books for me to read?"

Alexis turned toward her and planted a finger against her lips. "Shhhhhh!" she hushed firmly. "This is a library! You're supposed to be quiet!"

Megan winced. "I know you're supposed to be quiet," Megan said. "If you knew how to sign—if you knew sign language, I wouldn't have to make any sound at all!"

"Well, I don't know how to sign!" said Alexis.

"Well, you should!" said Megan.

"Stop talking to me," Alexis insisted.

Megan stepped back to consider the girl. Then she spoke, almost softly. "What's the matter with you?" she said. "Why are you so *mean* to me? All I've been is friendly toward you. It's because I'm deaf, right? You have a problem with me because I'm *deaf*."

Alexis's jaw dropped slightly, as if she were stunned. She turned toward Megan and gently licked her lips, as if about to speak. Megan didn't notice in the shadows of the library stacks, but the corners of Alexis's eyes had welled up slightly with the earliest trace of tears. "It's just—that I—," Alexis began, and then abruptly she pushed past Megan and kept walking until she had left the library.

Megan looked around to see if anyone had noticed what Alexis had just done to her. Alexis had just walked away from her and hadn't said "Excuse me" or anything when she pushed past. Alexis was the rudest, meanest girl that Megan had ever met.

Megan looked down at the book in her hands. A young girl was pictured on the cover, standing on an island beach and looking out to sea. But Megan didn't want to think about the book. She didn't even want to read it, now that Alexis had touched it. Megan put the book back on the shelf and went to ask the librarian for a different recommendation.

"What a shame," said Megan's mother. "I really thought you'd enjoy *Island of the Blue Dolphins*."

"It was checked out," said Megan with a shrug.

Lainee paused as she pushed the shopping cart through the wide lanes of the store and searched for signs of the party section.

"We don't have time to dawdle," Lainee said. "We have to pick up your brother from baseball practice, and I have to make supper."

"Excuse me," Megan said to a nearby stocking clerk, who looked up from a tremendous pyramid of cereal boxes.

"Yes, sorry to bother you," Lainee interjected, "but we're looking for party goods?"

"Aisle five," the stocking clerk replied.

"He said 'Aisle five,'" Lainee informed her daughter.

Megan huffed slightly and tossed her hair. "I

can read lips, mother!" she said with an edge of indignation. "Thank you very much!" She flipped her hand as though she didn't need her mother's assistance to do anything at all.

Lainee leaned forward so that Megan wouldn't miss her face. "You're such a brat," Lainee said, exaggerating the movement of her mouth. "Can you read that? You're such a brat sometimes. B-R-A-T. Brat."

Megan dropped her jaw in mock alarm and crossed her arms. She spun away and stormed down the aisle, stamping her feet as though she'd never been so insulted.

"Aisle five," Megan declared when she spotted the sign hanging over the party section. They had come in search of purple crepe paper and purple balloons. Megan was hoping that they would find a package of only-purple balloons so that they wouldn't have to pick the purple ones out of the packages of multi-colored balloons, or have to put red and blue ones together and "call it purple," which was what Matt had suggested they do.

At that moment a little boy came barreling around the corner, directly in the path of their shopping cart. "Look out, Mom!" cried Megan, jerking the cart to a halt.

The boy was about five years old with curly blond hair and a cute little potbelly. He was only a step away from their cart when he tripped over his own sneaker and, throwing his hands out to brace himself, landed hard on the linoleum.

"Ouch!" said Megan's mother. She stepped around the cart to help the little boy to his feet. "Did you hurt yourself?"

"Justin, Justin!" It was a girl's voice, calling down aisle three. Megan's mother turned to look for the aisle and seemed to acknowledge that it was someone who was responsible for the boy.

Megan was surprised to see that the girl was Alexis.

Alexis swooped down to scoop the curly-headed little boy off the ground. She hefted him against her hip with one arm tucked about his waist. "You can't run off like that, Justin," she said.

"Mom," said Megan. "This is Alexis."

"Oh!" said Megan's mother. "Alexis! Hello.

You're the new girl in Megan's school, right? Megan has told me so much about you."

"I can't really talk right now," said Alexis. She didn't even reach toward the handshake that Megan's mother offered. She hoisted the little boy into her arms and lurched into the distance.

As quickly as they had appeared, Alexis and the little boy disappeared down the aisle.

Megan noticed that her mother was still standing with her hand extended and her mouth hanging open.

"That was Alexis," said Megan, as though the facts spoke for themselves.

"And I suppose that was her little brother," Megan's mother added.

"I don't know," said Megan. "I don't know if she has a little brother. I don't know anything about her at all."

"Well, shy is one thing," said Megan's mother, "and rude is another."

"Now you see what I mean," Megan signed, and then she seized control of the shopping cart.

"You know me," said Megan's mother. "I'm

willing to give everyone the benefit of the doubt, but that Alexis is one tough cookie."

Megan was a little relieved that her mother had finally seen Alexis in action. She felt as though she wasn't crazy after all. It was like Megan's mother had said, Alexis wasn't so shy. Alexis was tough. Megan was glad that she wasn't coming to her birthday party.

Even so, as Megan passed aisle three, she couldn't help but glance down the aisle to catch sight of Alexis—the difficult girl with the difficult little boy.

6

Hats Off

MS. ENDEE HAD A THING FOR HOMEWORK.
Every afternoon before the bell rang, she
would review the day's homework assignment
in detail so that each student would know
what was expected the next morning. "And
there can be *no* excuses," she would add with a
wagging finger and a stern edge in her voice.
Jann used her attitude to mimic Ms. Endee's
stern tone as she translated the homework
assignment for Megan. She pursed her lips and
arched her eyebrows and delivered the message in short, choppy gestures.

Even though Ms. Endee could be strict, her homework assignments often had an element of fun. For example, Wednesday's homework assignment included three little words: Bring a hat. Ms. Endee refused to answer questions about the unusual assignment. "It's simple enough," she insisted. "Bring a hat."

"Bring a hat," Jann repeated in sign.

"Does it have to be *my* hat?" asked Tim Voss.

"Does it have to *fit?*" asked Casey.

"Questions, questions, questions," Ms. Endee blustered. She turned toward the whiteboard and wrote: "Bring a hat." "What part of 'bring a hat' don't you understand?" she asked the class.

"Does it have to be a *hat?*" asked Ronnie Jiu, but he was just trying to be funny.

"Yes, it has to be a hat," responded Ms. Endee, "but it doesn't say what size, what shape, what type, what color, what kind, or even *whose*. Do your math, do your English, read your social studies. And bring a hat. That's the assignment."

At that moment the bell rang. "And no

excuses!" Ms. Endee shouted as hordes of children charged the door.

On Thursday morning Ms. Endee got what she asked for. Her classroom looked like a crazy hat shop. Kids wore big floppy garden hats, sparkling sombreros, favorite baseball caps, cowboy hats, Chinese coolie hats, and construction helmets. There were sailor hats and skipper caps and even a couple berets. Ronnie Jiu wore his mother's shower cap. "Hey, it's a *hat*," Ronnie protested.

Megan wore a pith helmet that her dad used when they went hiking. Cindy wore an old-fashioned nurse's cap that once belonged to her grandmother.

Ms. Endee stood in front of the room wearing a graduation cap: a flat black mortarboard with a bright gold tassel. As the class giggled in their seats, their teacher reached into the big drawer of her desk and pulled out a white lab coat. When she pulled it on, she looked like a really smart scientist.

Jann wore a Statue of Liberty crown with green pointy spires. When she signed "Good morning" to Megan, she clasped a dictionary under one arm, pretending to hold a tablet like the statue.

"I'm glad to see everyone wore their *thinking caps* today," Ms. Endee announced, as though the crazy hats had been simply a happy coincidence, "because it is time to announce this year's teams for the annual science fair."

The class tittered and applauded. The science fair was a particularly exciting event at Wilmot Elementary because the faculty approached it with a sense of fun. First, second, and third-place prizes—blue, red, and green ribbons—were awarded to the real science fair winners based on scientific merit and achievement. But the wackier experiments were also honored so that kids who weren't wizards at science would get involved as well. Mr. Ryan awarded prizes for the silliest projects, the goofiest projects, and he awarded the special Deep Space Award for the most unusual project—the one that was really "out there."

The students squirmed excitedly in their seats. Cindy couldn't stop giggling, and Megan gripped the far edge of her desktop as if she were bracing herself for her desk to blast off.

Ms. Endee reached into the pocket of her lab coat and revealed the list of this year's collaborators. Before she read the list, she referred to the whiteboard, where she had already written the word "collaboration" in big red letters. "I'm going to assign teams for the science fair," she explained. "You'll be working together as a *team*. You're going to *collaborate*." She tapped the word "collaboration" on the board with her red marker.

Ms. Endee was big on collaboration. The students had collaborated in teams the previous fall when they had built a colonial village on the playground just before Thanksgiving. "You're going to practice *collaboration*," she reiterated while she tapped.

Cindy leaned toward Megan. "*Collaboration!* I get it already," she signed. "Get on with the list!"

"Who remembers the first rule of collaboration?" Ms. Endee asked the class.

Hands shot into the air. Megan jumped out of her seat with her hand extended. Cindy did too.

"Yes, Cindy," said Ms. Endee.

"'Say yes!'" said Cindy, rather pleased with herself for remembering.

"That's right," said Ms. Endee. "If someone suggests an idea, you have to 'say yes.' Any idea is a good idea. And what's the second rule of collaboration?"

Megan jumped out of her seat again, trying to get Ms. Endee's attention. "Call on me!" she cried anxiously. "Call on me!"

"Someone I haven't called on yet," said her teacher.

"Please!" Megan begged. "Oh, please!"

"All right, Megan," said Ms. Endee.

Megan leaned forward against her desk. "Make believe your collaborator is your new best friend," she said and signed, both at the same time. She smiled at Cindy. Even though they were officially best friends, both Cindy and Megan had already learned to work with other kids on collaboration projects. In the colonial village last fall Megan had worked with Tracy on a spinning-wheel display, and Cindy had worked with a boy she barely knew named Donny Vargas on a makeshift butter churn. Megan and Cindy hadn't been able to work together the way they'd wanted, but it had still been a lot of fun.

"That's right," said Ms. Endee, pleased with the response. "Make believe your collaborator is your new best friend. That way—we do what?"

"Get the job done!" the class chimed together.

Megan happened to glance sideways and notice that Alexis was sitting quietly. She hadn't chimed in with the other classmates because she probably hadn't known the answer. Alexis probably didn't know the rules of collaboration. *Probably the first time Alexis didn't know the right answer*, Megan thought with a dismissive sniff.

Ms. Endee clapped her hands to call the class to attention. "I'm going to call out two names for each team," she said, "and I want you to sit with your partner—using *library voices*—and discuss two or three ideas for science fair projects. Then tomorrow you get to run those ideas past Mr. Ryan."

The kids were crazy about Mr. Ryan, the

school science teacher. He looked a little bit like a mad scientist because he had frizzy red hair, big thick eyeglasses, and broad bushy eyebrows with wild hairs that went in every direction. But all the kids agreed he was incredibly smart and really very funny.

The classroom fell silent as Ms. Endee read the names. Cindy was paired right off the bat with Tony Rosenblum. Kaitlyn got matched with a quiet boy named Sawyer.

Megan waited patiently—well, almost patiently—as kids' names were called. In a very short while almost everyone had been paired up.

Megan didn't mind the wait. Not really. It added to the excitement. At least that's what she told herself. But at some point Megan noticed that her name hadn't been called yet. And she noticed that Alexis's name hadn't been called yet either.

Megan didn't talk about it much, but sometimes she thought she was psychic. It didn't happen all the time, but occasionally Megan found she could predict what was going to happen before it actually did. It was only a crazy thought. But even as Megan imagined it, she felt certain it would come to pass.

Oh, no! thought Megan. *Ms. Endee is going to match me with Alexis.*

Megan's eyes darted toward Alexis just in time to notice that Alexis had been glancing at Megan. It couldn't be a coincidence. Megan was more certain than ever that her premonition was true.

By this point the names had whittled down to only four kids without partners, and Megan was fairly numb with expectation. Tracy was also in the last four names, but Megan knew she wouldn't get matched with Tracy because they'd already collaborated on the colonial spinning wheel, and Ms. Endee had a way of keeping tabs on her collaborators.

Cindy signed across the room, "Are you okay?" but Megan looked away, too upset to respond.

Sure enough, Tracy was matched with a nice girl named Maya. After that, Ms. Endee didn't even need to say the words. Megan didn't even need to watch Jann's translation to know what was coming.

It was obvious. Megan was stuck with Alexis. She had been paired with the meanest and most difficult stuck-up, annoying girl in the entire fourth grade!

Now that the list had been read, collaborators were supposed to meet at each other's desks to discuss potential science fair ideas— but instead of meeting Alexis at her desk, Megan flagged Jann to meet her at Ms. Endee's desk. Megan marched directly to the front of the classroom and right up to Ms. Endee.

"I can't work with her," she signed, jerking a thumb toward Alexis.

Ms. Endee waited for a moment for Jann to translate Megan's words into speech. "Why not?" asked Ms. Endee.

"Because she *hates* me," Megan signed. "Alexis *hates* me."

Ms. Endee flinched slightly before she responded. She glanced toward the back of the classroom where Alexis sat quietly at her desk, flipping through the pages of a notebook.

"'Hate' is a very strong word," said Ms. Endee. "We shouldn't use that word unless we mean it."

"Even so, she hates me," Megan repeated.

"Alexis?" said Ms. Endee in a disbelieving tone. "Alexis doesn't hate you. She can't possibly *hate* you. She's only been here three days!"

"She hates me," Megan insisted. "She really, really hates me."

"Has she ever *said* that she hates you?"

Megan twisted her lips and sighed. It was true that Alexis hadn't exactly said anything like that. "Not exactly," she responded. "But I can tell she hates me! She's mean to me. She ignores me. And she scrunches her nose when she has to look at me. Ask Alexis if you don't believe me. She'll tell you I'm right."

Ms. Endee shook her head emphatically. She wasn't having it. "Megan," she began, "you're one of the brighter and more responsible students in this class. You and Alexis should be able to work together. There's no reason in the world why you two can't get along."

"It's not that *I* don't get along with *her*," Megan insisted. "It's that *she* doesn't get along with *me*."

"Megan, I expect you to make this collaboration work. I'm not reassigning science fair partners based on a popularity contest. I expect you and Alexis to put aside your differences and do the work at hand."

"Yes, Ms. Endee," Megan said obediently, even though she wasn't feeling particularly obedient at all. She felt a little ashamed for complaining about Alexis in the first place, but mostly she felt disappointed by the prospect of being matched with the mean girl as a science fair partner. Clearly she was stuck with Alexis whether she liked it or not.

Ms. Endee set aside the last hour of the school day for the students to meet with their collaborators and brainstorm ideas. As Megan glanced about, she noticed the other students were chattering animatedly. She saw Tracy and Maya talking, deep into plans for a project titled "Snails: Friend or Foe?" Kaitlyn and Sawyer had decided to examine "Why Some Dogs Prefer Cat Food over Dog Food." Rainbows, constellations, and magnets were as popular as ever.

Ms. Endee smiled at all the commotion. Normally, she would have asked the students to keep the volume down, but she was pleased with the lively exchange of ideas around the classroom.

Megan and Alexis, on the other hand, sat in silence.

"I don't know how to talk to you," Megan said at last.

"I don't know how to talk to you, either," Alexis replied, apparently satisfied with the stalemate.

Megan didn't expect the conversation to go any further, but then, to her surprise, Alexis continued. "Last year when I went to school in Houston," she abruptly blurted, "I did a science fair project about the tide. Every afternoon I went to the beach and I measured the tide."

"That won't work here," said Megan. "We don't have an ocean."

"It wasn't an ocean," said Alexis. "It was the Gulf of Mexico."

"Whatever," said Megan, flipping a hand.

"Well, *you* come up with an idea," said Alexis.

"I'm trying," Megan said with annoyance. "Nothing's coming up."

Alexis bent to the side to reach under her desk for her pencil pouch. Megan couldn't help but notice that the pencil pouch was purple.

"You like purple?" she asked Alexis.

"It's all right," said Alexis, without a great deal of enthusiasm. She pulled a novelty pencil out of her pouch—a double-thick pencil with shiny foil squares up and down the sides. Megan noticed that the pencil was purple too.

"You like purple more than you think," Megan offered.

Alexis only shrugged. She wrote her e-mail address on a piece of paper and handed it to Megan. "Here's my e-mail," she said. "Shoot me a message if you come up with an idea later."

"We're supposed to do this *together*," said Megan. "I'm not supposed to do your work for you."

"I'm not asking you to," Alexis protested. "I just figured we should stay in touch."

Megan sighed dramatically. This collaboration was doomed. At that moment Cindy crashed their meeting, slamming herself against Megan's desk with a cheery "Oops, sorry!" Then she said, "Sooooo, how's it going?"

"Awful," said Megan. "We don't have a single idea. How about you?"

"Tony Rosenblum and I have got it all planned," said Cindy. "We're comparing the absorption rate of different diapers. It's kind of disgusting but also kind of perfect because Tony Rosenblum has a new baby brother and an endless supply of disposable diapers."

"Perfect," said Megan. "Lu-cky."

Alexis tapped her purple pencil against the desktop but didn't say a word.

Megan looked at Cindy and shrugged. The situation was hopeless.

By the time the bell rang, Megan and Alexis still didn't have any ideas.

"Look," said Alexis, in an exasperated last-ditch effort the moment before everyone hit the door, "let's both come up with an idea tonight, and tomorrow we'll vote on which one is our favorite."

"That won't work," said Megan. "You'll vote for your idea and I'll vote for mine."

"Good point," Alexis allowed. "But maybe we'll put our ideas together."

"I don't think that's going to happen," said Megan with a dismissive flip of her hand.

"Good-bye class," cried Ms. Endee. "See you tomorrow!"

Megan smiled at Ms. Endee and turned back to see that Alexis had loaded her purple pencil back into the purple pouch, had grabbed her backpack, and was already headed for the door—without even saying good-bye.

"It's not going to work," said Megan, looking at Cindy. "I'm being nice, but she's being totally difficult."

7

Surprise Purple

MEGAN HAD FIVE COOKBOOKS OPEN ON THE counter and was buried in the index of the sixth.

Matt walked into the kitchen and announced himself with a hearty belch.

"Ugh!" Megan groaned, disgusted at the smell and fanning the air with the open cookbook.

"What are you doing?" Matt asked.

"Nothing," Megan said with exasperation. "Because I can't find it in the cookbook."

"Can't find what?" asked Matt. "What are

you trying to make?" He circled the counter to lean over Megan's shoulder and focus on the cookbook.

"I'm looking for a recipe for purple frosting for my purple birthday cake," said Megan. "But I looked under *f* for frosting and *p* for purple and I couldn't find *anything*." She snapped the cookbook shut. "Okay," she allowed, "there are recipes listed under frosting but nothing that says 'purple frosting.'"

"You make purple frosting out of eggplant," Matt suggested. "Try looking under 'eggplant.'"

Megan looked suspicious. "Will that work?" she asked, reaching for the cookbook once more.

"Eggplant frosting, my favorite!" Matt cried. "I used to beg Mom to make that all the time! She'd put it on cupcakes and I'd be the hero of the first grade."

Megan eyed Matt with greater suspicion. Sarcasm was difficult to detect when a person was signing, but she was fairly convinced that Matt was being sarcastic.

Matt turned his back on Megan and walked

to the cupboard. He returned to smack a box of food colors onto the counter directly in front of Megan.

"What's this?" Megan asked.

"Food coloring, Einstein," said Matt.

"I thought of that already," Megan protested, "but food coloring doesn't have purple." She pushed the box away. "Food coloring has only red and blue and green and yellow."

"Einstein," Matt nagged. "Red and blue *make* purple."

"I know that," Megan snapped automatically, but then she brightened considerably. Megan hated being corrected, but she prided herself on being able to admit her mistakes. It hadn't even occurred to her to mix the colors. "Of course!" Megan cried. "Red and blue make purple!" She lifted the red and the blue bottles from the box and shook them so that the dye sloshed inside. "Are you allowed to do that?" she asked Matt. "Is it really okay if you mix the colors?"

"Moms do it all the time," said Matt. "But I don't see why you want purple frosting, anyway.

People aren't going to like it. You're only going to make their tongues purple."

"Some people like purple tongues," Megan insisted. "I know I do." She was thinking of grape Popsicles in the summertime or grape lollipops at the doctor's office and the way they always gave kids a chance to show off their tongues. She headed for the sink to add a quick splash of water to a juice glass.

"*Blech,*" said Matt, scrunching his face. "You might as well stick with the eggplant frosting. Face it, Megan. Not everybody likes purple!"

"But some people *do,*" Megan argued. She dripped two drops of red food coloring into the water and watched it dissolve. The water quickly turned a rosy shade of pink. She added two drops of blue. The colors swirled separately for a moment before Megan stuck her finger into the glass to give the solution a quick twirl.

"See, it's purple," said Matt, leaning forward to look at the purple water. "Just like I told you."

"Funny how you think red and blue won't get along," said Megan. "Then you mix them together and—surprise! Purple!"

"And not a bad purple," said Matt, considering the water. "It's more violet, really."

"See?" said Megan. "That proves it! People *think* they don't like purple, and then they see it, and they love it!"

"That's not what I said," Matt protested. "I didn't say I loved it." But Megan had already leaped from the kitchen stool and thrown both hands into the air. She danced about as though she'd just been struck by the absolutely most excellent, most extraordinary, most brilliant idea.

"That's it! I've got it!" Megan cried.

"Got what?"

"My science fair project!" said Megan. "I'm going to prove that purple is the greatest color of them all!" She gestured at the purple water. "See? See?" she asked. "Is this not the greatest science fair project idea of all time?"

"Hmm, yeah," said Matt, dripping with sarcasm. "Sounds like the Nobel Prize to me."

The following day Mr. Ryan visited Ms. Endee's fourth-grade classroom to approve the science fair projects. Kids were generally encouraged to be creative with their experiments, but some kids needed guidance down more realistic paths. Melinda Bird and Kim Lewis, for example, wanted to build a rain forest by the school Dumpster.

"That's a really great idea," said Mr. Ryan, "but a rain forest takes a lot of dirt and a whole lot of trees."

"I told you so," said Kim to Melinda. "Too much dirt, too many trees, *and* too much water. Rain forests need lots of water. It's a *rain* forest. Hello?"

"And how is the Dumpster truck going to reach the Dumpster if there's a rain forest in the way?" asked Mr. Ryan.

"Okay, okay," said Melinda. "We can build a suspension bridge instead." Kim smiled because the suspension bridge had been her idea.

"A suspension bridge?" Mr. Ryan arched his eyebrows. "Where are you going to build that? In the school parking lot?"

"Just a little one," Kim insisted. "Out of Popsicle sticks."

Mr. Ryan brushed his hand across his forehead and issued a big "Whew!" as though he were really relieved.

Other kids, like Megan and Alexis, for example, needed help figuring out how to agree on any idea at all.

"Let me get this straight. 'Purple is the greatest color.'" Mr. Ryan repeated Megan's words. "How do you plan to prove that?"

"Just, I don't know, ask people," said Megan. "We'll conduct a survey."

"Uh-*huh*," Mr. Ryan said, scratching his chin. In sign language Mr. Ryan was saying "old man" but Megan knew from the context of the conversation that he was simply thinking of a response. And she could tell by looking at him that he wasn't sold on the idea of purple. "Not really much of an experiment," he added.

"Well, it's the only idea I had," said Megan. She was determined to make it work even if she had to be stubborn to do it.

"Okay, hmmm," Mr. Ryan said, turning toward Megan's partner. "What's your idea, Alexis?"

Megan sulked. *Here we go*, she thought. *Mr. Ryan's going to like Alexis's idea better than mine.*

"Hamsters," said Alexis. "I like hamsters."

"*Hamsters?*" blurted Megan. She brushed a finger across the tip of her nose almost like she was scratching whiskers. The gesture was sign language for the word "hamster."

"Yes," Alexis insisted. "Hamsters." She pointed beyond Mr. Ryan to the hamster cage that Ms. Endee kept on the ledge behind her desk. The school hamster, known as Zippity, was a brown and white fur ball. At present he was curled in a ball, apparently asleep, at the bottom of the rodent wheel.

Mr. Ryan arched one of his wild eyebrows at Alexis. "Oh, sure," he said, "all the kids love Zippity. Everybody loves the fur ball." He leaned closer and tapped his pencil against a notepad. "But what is it about hamsters that makes them a good science fair project? What are you thinking?"

"I was just thinking a project about *hamsters*," said Alexis. "What they eat and what they are and what they do and stuff." She was afraid to say too much about her idea because she was afraid Megan would jump all over it.

And Megan did. "What is that? Isn't that just like a book report on hamsters?" Megan asked. She flung her hands dismissively. "That's not much of an experiment either," she said.

"No, it's not, really," Mr. Ryan agreed. "Although I understand completely because I am quite fond of Zippity myself." He lifted one hand and scratched his head. In sign language he was saying, "I'm thinking." Which was exactly what he was doing.

Megan and Alexis looked at each other.

"Hamsters," insisted Alexis.

"Purple," insisted Megan.

"Hamsters!" said Alexis.

"Purple!" said Megan.

"I suppose . . . ," said Mr. Ryan, interrupting the battle. He tapped his finger against his lip. In sign language it meant "be quiet," but Mr. Ryan meant "listen to me." "I suppose," he repeated, dragging out the word because he was still thinking even as he spoke.

Megan and Alexis stopped bickering and waited for Mr. Ryan to get to the point.

"I suppose," Mr. Ryan said, thinking and tapping, "you could do *both*."

"Both?" said the girls in unison.

"Maybe you could study what hamsters think of purple. What's their favorite color? Although I have to say we can't exactly interview Zippity. I know because I've tried." Mr. Ryan leaned toward Zippity with an imaginary microphone. "Hello, Zippity?" he said. "Zippity? Hello?"

Zippity didn't even look up.

The girls giggled at the sight of Mr. Ryan interviewing Zippity with a microphone. The laughter helped get them over their problem.

"Maybe," said Megan, "we could color the hamster's food purple, and see if he eats it." She was thinking of the red and blue food coloring, of course. Megan had quickly become an expert at mixing food colors to create purple. Just last night Megan's mother had to insist at supper that nobody wanted to try purple mashed potatoes.

"Purple hamster food," said Alexis. *"Ick."*

"I know, *ick*," agreed Mr. Ryan. "And hamsters only eat hamster food, so coloring it purple wouldn't really prove anything."

The girls fell silent for a moment.

"Maybe," said Alexis, "we could give him

the choice between a purple something and a different-colored something."

"That might work," said Mr. Ryan.

"Like *balloons*," suggested Megan. She was thinking, of course, of the purple balloons she had bought for her birthday party—a great big bag of them—that night she saw Alexis at the store being so nasty to her cute little brother. "We could ask the hamster to choose between a red balloon and a purple balloon."

"Hmmm," said Alexis, not sold on the balloons.

"I know, hmmm," echoed Mr. Ryan, not so sold on the idea himself.

"Or what about *rooms*?" suggested Megan, shooting from the hip. "A hamster could choose between different-colored rooms."

"You mean like *classrooms*?" asked Mr. Ryan.

"Maybe," said Megan. "I don't know." She kind of doubted that they'd be able to convince Ms. Endee to let them paint the classroom purple.

"What about hamster-size rooms?" suggested Alexis.

Hamster-size rooms, thought Megan. She had to admit that it wasn't a bad idea.

"But how do you get the hamster from one room to the other?" asked Mr. Ryan. "Are you just going to drop Zippity into a room and see how he reacts? Or are you going to give him a choice?"

"A *maze!*" cried Megan. "Let's build him a *maze!*"

"A maze that leads to two or three different rooms," added Alexis, already into the idea.

"And we can watch Zippity in the maze and keep track of how many times he goes to one room over another!" said Megan.

"We'll keep a chart!" said Alexis.

The girls looked to Mr. Ryan for approval.

Mr. Ryan was already smiling. "Sounds like a science fair project to me," he said.

Megan and Alexis met at a patio table outside the school library to hash out their ideas for the science fair project. Mr. Ryan had already agreed to let them take Zippity home in his cage for the weekend so that they could run him through the maze after it was built. "But you better not lose him," Mr. Ryan said, after he poked the sleeping hamster with a finger as a way of saying good-bye. "Principal Smelter will have my hide if he finds out I lost Zippity." The girls solemnly promised to take good care of the hamster over the weekend. The only problem was that they still didn't have a maze.

"I've never built a maze before," said Megan. "Have you?"

"I've never built one," said Alexis, "but I was *inside* a maze once. It was a garden maze, so it was made out of hedges."

Because Alexis didn't know sign language, Megan had to rely on her lip-reading skills. But she understood Alexis well enough. "Cool," Megan replied. "I saw a maze like that once in a movie. You get *lost* in a maze like that."

"I liked it at first," said Alexis, "but then it got scary and all I wanted was to get out."

"I was in a maze at the school carnival," said Megan, "but it was made out of bed sheets and clothesline. It was like getting lost in the laundry."

Alexis laughed.

"But we can't use a garden maze or a carnival maze with a hamster," said Megan. "Zippity would bust right through the bushes and sheets."

"A maze *that* big is too big for a hamster."

"Exactly," said Megan. "And too big for the science fair."

"It's probably going to end up being about this big," said Alexis. She stretched her arms to roughly the size of a card table.

"And made of cardboard or something," said Megan. "Like a big box. Big and flat."

"Where are we going to find a big, flat box?" asked Alexis.

"Beats me," said Megan. "The only thing I ever made out of a box was a diorama."

"Me too!" chimed Alexis. "I made it out of a shoe box."

"Me too," Megan chimed back. "I love dioramas."

"Me too," said Alexis.

The process of brainstorming their hamster-size maze got stalled once the girls discovered a shared passion for dioramas. "Mine was the

Salem witch trials," said Megan. "I still have it."

"Cool," said Alexis. "Mine was the swallows returning to San Juan Capistrano."

"Cool," said Megan. She was trying to picture Alexis's diorama and her own. "Isn't it amazing what you can do with a shoe box?"

"Absolutely," Alexis agree.

Megan and Alexis were both quiet for a moment. It would be hard to say which one came up with the idea first. Maybe the idea occurred to each girl at the exact same time. Regardless, it was a mere instant before the girls looked at each other and cried, "Shoe boxes!"

"We could build the whole maze out of shoe boxes!"

"But won't that take too many?"

"Not really," said Alexis. She sketched a design on scratch paper to demonstrate how they could build the whole thing with interlocking shoe boxes. Megan offered suggestions as to where the different-colored rooms should go. They agreed that it was no fair putting hamster food in the purple room because that would give purple an unfair advantage over red and blue, the colors they had chosen for the other two rooms. However, they did think it was a good idea to put a little hamster food at different corners of the maze so that Zippity had some reason to travel from one end of the maze to the other.

Megan did a rough calculation and guessed that eight shoeboxes would do the job. Alexis knew her mom had sharp sewing scissors they could use to cut the interlocking slots and hamster-size doorways in the shoe boxes. Megan knew her father had thick masking tape in the garage that they could use to hold the shoe boxes together. Megan, of course, had purple paint, and Alexis was pretty sure that she had red and blue.

"So we're all set," said Alexis.

"Wait," said Megan. "What about shoe boxes? *Eight* shoe boxes! Will we have enough?"

"Eight is a lot of shoe boxes," said Alexis.

"That's why I brought it up," said Megan.

That October, when Megan had been required to do a diorama of colonial days for class, she had put the project off until the last possible minute and, naturally, couldn't find a single usable shoe box in the entire house. She only managed to score a decent-size box for her witch-burning tableau because she convinced her mother to hit the mall for a new pair of high heels. Megan couldn't imagine that she'd be able to convince her mom to buy *eight* new pairs of shoes so they could build their hamster maze that night.

"I have a brother," Alexis said shyly, looking in the other direction so that Megan wasn't sure what to make of the comment.

"Yeah," said Megan. "That little kid. I met him at the store."

"He likes sneakers, but he grows through them," said Alexis.

"Brothers are like that," said Megan.

"But he never gets rid of his old sneakers," Alexis continued, "and he never gets rid of the *boxes*."

Megan nodded slowly, catching on to the point that Alexis was making. "*Fee-fi-fo-fum*," said Megan, "I smell shoe boxes."

"That's what I'm thinking," said Alexis.

"But your kid brother is still little," Megan observed. "Won't those boxes be too small?"

"Big enough for a hamster, maybe," said Alexis.

Megan had to agree. "But you know what?" Megan continued. "My brother is the exact same way. He doesn't like me in his room, but I bet he's got every pair of sneakers he ever owned—still in the box, still in his closet."

"Four shoe boxes from you, four shoe boxes from me?" asked Alexis.

"Deal," said Megan. "That should do it. I'll go home and get my brother's boxes and meet you at your house."

Alexis flinched. "Actually," she said, "it's not such a good idea to meet at *my* house."

"But my house is crazy," Megan responded. "Everything is turned upside down because we're in the middle of preparations for my birthday party." Megan caught herself at the mention of her own party—the very same party that Alexis had already announced her intention *not* to attend. But Alexis didn't seem to notice the remark at all.

"No, no," said Alexis. "That's okay. Your house is a much better idea."

"Are you sure your house wouldn't be easier?" Megan insisted.

"No, really," said Alexis. "Besides, I want to see your house."

Megan smiled. She was happy to show her house to Alexis. It was almost like they were becoming friends. But why was Alexis so worried about Megan visiting her house? *That's crazy*, thought Megan. *Why wouldn't she want me to see her house?*

"But I want to see your house too," said Megan.

"It's just that," Alexis continued, "we just moved and we're still moving and everything is *new*—so the whole house is upside-down with moving boxes and all."

Megan realized that Alexis was probably right. "So *my* upside-down house or *your* upside-down house?" she asked.

"Yours," Alexis insisted. "Your house. Really. It would be much, much better."

"Okay," said Megan. She reached for a pencil and wrote her address on the corner of their design for the maze. "Come over as soon as you can."

"As soon as I get the boxes," said Alexis.

Matt kept a sign from the hardware store tacked to his bedroom door that read: KEEP OUT. Underneath the stern warning, Matt had used a big red marker to scrawl "And that means *you*, Megan!"

Megan approached the door to Matt's bedroom and didn't give the sign a second thought before she grabbed the doorknob and pushed open the door.

The door didn't exactly open all the way. Matt's room was the usual mess. Heaps of clothes were piled on the floor. Basically, it looked like the laundry hamper had exploded. Cardboard boxes were loaded with toys that Matt refused to get rid of even though he didn't play with them anymore. Megan found a path across the room, sidestepping the discarded comic books and abandoned sporting goods. She reached the closet, shoved the sliding door, and switched on the light.

Megan looked down and was relieved to

find exactly what she wanted. Shoe boxes, and plenty of them. She dropped onto her haunches and began tossing Matt's old sneakers into a tangled clump by the closet door, and then she stacked the empty boxes into a nice, neat pile. She used one hand to pinch her nose firmly shut during the process because Matt's old sneakers smelled really bad.

Truly disgusting, Megan thought to herself. *Absolutely repulsive.*

Megan whirled about when she felt Matt tap her shoulder.

"What are you doing in my room?" he demanded.

"I'm cleaning out your closet," Megan replied, trying to sound as helpful as possible even though she was still pinching her nose.

"You're throwing out my shoes!" Matt exclaimed.

"No, I'm not," said Megan. "They're right there." She pointed at the tattered sneakers heaped on top of one another. She reached for a container of foot powder on the floor beside Matt's bureau and sprinkled it over the mass of shoes. "You should air them out,"

Megan continued, trying to sound helpful. "Your shoes are too stinky."

"Leave my shoes alone," Matt cried. He seized the foot powder container from her hands and tossed it on top of the bureau.

"But I need your shoe boxes!" Megan protested.

"Not another diorama," Matt said with a groan.

"No, this time it's a science fair," Megan replied.

"I like my shoes in boxes," Matt insisted.

"You're so ridiculous," Megan argued. "Nobody keeps shoes in their boxes. You're supposed to get rid of the boxes. Besides, this is for *science*."

"What are you doing?" Matt asked.

"We're making a maze for a hamster to run in," said Megan.

"Cool!" said Matt, without any more argument. "You can have the boxes if I get to watch."

"Not a problem."

"Who are you making the maze with?" Matt asked.

"Alexis," said Megan, not thinking anything of it.

"Alexis!" said Matt. "You mean the new girl who's not very nice?"

"She's nice enough," said Megan.

"You said she was *mean* before," said Matt.

"So I was wrong," said Megan. "Anyway, she's my science fair partner."

"Wait, wait!" Matt cried. "I've got it! The best science fair project in the world! We'll lock you and the mean girl in the same room! See which one survives!"

"Funny, funny," said Megan. She applied herself to counting shoe boxes. She had three. She flung one last pair of sneakers onto the pile and seized the empty box.

"Hey!" Matt protested.

"That's all," said Megan. "Only four boxes. We're hooking them together to build our maze."

"Why don't you use a packing box that already has compartments for all the jars and glasses?" Matt suggested. "That way you can use the compartments to make corridors and rooms. And you can leave my shoe boxes alone."

Megan hesitated. The packing box idea was a good one. *But it's not the idea that Alexis and I came up with*, she resolved.

"Because Alexis and I are using shoe boxes!" she declared. With that, she scooped up her boxes and headed downstairs.

"So," said Matt, "the mysterious Alexis!"

"What's that supposed to mean?" asked Alexis. She was standing on the doorstep with four shoe boxes and a small hamster cage.

"Nothing," said Matt. "I'll get Megan." He left the door open for Alexis to step inside as he thundered upstairs, taking two steps at a time. Alexis stepped into the hall and peeked at the doorways to the left and right. A moment later Megan and Matt were charging downstairs together in a wild romp, like puppies in a field.

"I win!" said Megan when she landed in the front hall after jumping the last three steps.

"Only by a nose," said Matt.

"That's my brother," Megan said to Alexis, pointing at her brother.

"We met," said Alexis. "Hey."

"Hey," Matt said back.

"We're working in the dining room," Megan urged, tugging on Alexis's sleeve. "You brought Zippity?"

"Is that the hamster?" asked Matt.

"Looks like one," said Alexis, holding up the cage.

"Is it dead or is it asleep?" asked Matt, eyeing the chunky fuzz ball inside the cage.

"He likes to *sleep*," said Megan. "Just like *you*." She pushed Matt so that he would get out of their way, and led Alexis into the dining room so they could get to work on their project.

It took a lot to surprise Megan's mother, so she hardly reacted at all when she entered the dining room to find Megan and another girl kneeling on the dining room chairs, huddled over the table, assembling and reassembling shoe boxes in various patterns. Lainee wasn't even particularly surprised by the hamster cage on the table, although she wasn't happy about it either.

"Can we get the hamster cage off the dining room table?" Lainee announced, more as a command than a question.

"His name is Zippity," said Megan. "Oh, and you remember Alexis." She jerked her head toward the girl kneeling on the next chair.

It was Alexis's presence in the dining room that caught Lainee by surprise. *"Alexis,"* she said, almost singsong with wonder. She bobbed her head curiously and smiled politely, letting Megan know that she expected to hear the full story later.

"Alexis and I are doing a science fair project," said Megan.

"A hamster maze, Mrs. Merrill," Alexis explained. "With one purple room."

"One purple room," repeated Lainee. "Well, that doesn't surprise me." She crossed her arms for a moment, watching the two girls at work, and decided it was probably the wrong time to make them clear the dining room table. Zippity was still asleep in his cage, but even so, a hamster was still a hamster. She tapped Megan to make sure she had her attention, and signed, "I'm going to need the table back in half an hour."

"Okay, Mom," said Megan. Megan had been applying masking tape to a pair of boxes.

Alexis was using big shears to cut a hamster-size doorway.

"Be careful with those scissors," added Lainee.

"Okay, Mrs. Merrill," said Alexis.

Lainee eyed the bag of purple feathers resting on the sideboard. "Megan, I asked you twice already to put this bag of purple feathers away before it gets knocked over and we have purple feathers everywhere."

"*Okay*, Mom! I'll take care of it," Megan snapped, hoping her mother would drop the subject. She didn't want to mention the purple feathers or the invitations to the Positively Purple Party in front of Alexis.

Lainee lifted the hamster cage off the table with one finger. "And Zippity," she said, eyeing the fuzz ball inside, "goes *off* the table."

Megan scooped the cage out of her mother's hands and placed it on the carpet in the corner.

"Should we put purple feathers in the purple room?" Alexis asked after Lainee had left the dining room. She lifted the bag of feathers off the sideboard and studied the contents.

"That's an idea," said Megan. "But then wouldn't we have to put red feathers in the red room and blue feathers in the blue room?"

"Forget I mentioned it," said Alexis.

"Too much bother," said Megan.

"Just an idea," said Alexis. She dropped the bag back onto the sideboard, and Megan promptly forgot about the purple feathers altogether.

It took most of the half hour to assemble the boxes, get the doorways to line up, tape the boxes together, and paint the red, blue, and purple rooms. By that point, they agreed, it was time to quit. They would have to "run" Zippity through the maze in the morning.

"Come over tomorrow," said Megan.

"I have ballet class on Saturday morning," said Alexis, "but I could come over after that."

"Sounds good."

"Hopefully he'll be *awake*," said Alexis, nudging Zippity's cage.

"Maybe we should feed him a lot of sugar and get him all wired," said Megan. Both of them laughed. They lifted the hamster maze off the table and set it on its side against the dining room wall.

"I better call home for a ride," said Alexis, spanking her hands clean.

"The telephone's in the kitchen," said Megan. "Follow me."

In the kitchen Megan's mom was tearing open a box of pasta and pouring it into a pot of boiling water. Lainee made eye contact with Megan while Alexis was on the telephone and rolled her eyes in a way that meant "Soooo—?"

In response, Megan clenched her jaw, cocked her head, and crossed her eyeballs in a way that meant "Can't explain now, Mom!"

Alexis replaced the telephone in its cradle and announced, "My dad's gonna drive by in about five minutes."

"I'll wait outside with you," Megan offered.

"You don't have to," said Alexis.

"I don't mind," said Megan. She tugged on Alexis's sleeve to lead her toward the front door.

"Bye, Alexis!" Lainee called from the stove. She was stirring the pasta with a big wooden spoon.

"Good-bye, Mrs. Merrill," said Alexis.

The two girls left the room, and Megan's mother smiled.

Outside, it was not exactly dark yet, although the sun had set.

"Look," said Megan, nudging Alexis and pointing at the sky, "*purple!*"

She and Alexis were sitting on the front step, waiting for Alexis's dad to show up in his car. Alexis looked up at the sky and smiled. "I'm glad we're doing the purple," she said.

"I'm glad we're doing the hamster," said Megan. And she smiled too.

They were both quiet after that, although Megan clutched her knees to her chest and it was a while before she lost her little smile. She didn't know how to explain to her mom how things had gotten easier with Alexis, but it was funny to think that she had a hamster to thank.

8

Gesundheit

"AAAAHHH-CHOO!"

Megan didn't hear Matt sneeze, but she could tell that he had by the way he gripped the dining room table and scrambled for his napkin. His hair rattled and his face scrunched as his head bounced forward. Megan saw her mom admonish Matt to turn away or sneeze into his sleeve, and she saw her dad say "Gesundheit!" So she knew it was a sneeze.

Typical, thought Megan. She was in the middle of explaining her science fair project to her dad and she didn't like to be interrupted. She had already explained to her dad the whole story about the new girl at school who was really perfect—but really difficult—and how she, Megan, had got stuck doing her science fair project with the girl. She said, "Gesundheit, Matt" to acknowledge Matt's sneeze, and went back to her story. She was deep into the science fair project itself at this point. "And one room is red and one room is blue, but the nicest room is purple."

"A purple room?" her dad asked, somewhat disbelieving.

"Aaaahhh-choo!"

It was Matt again.

"Gesundheit, Matt!" said her dad.

"Goodness gracious, Matt," said Lainee. "Are you catching a cold?"

"If you're getting sick or something, could you not sneeze on me?" said Megan to Matt. "I've got a big weekend planned. I have to run the hamster through the maze—"

"A hamster through a maze?" her dad asked, still somewhat disbelieving.

"So I really don't want to catch Matt's cold!" Megan insisted.

"I've got a big weekend too," said Matt, sniffling and wiping his nose. "This is my baseball tryout weekend! I can't afford to be sick!"

"It's probably just dust," said Lainee. "You were perfectly fine earlier."

"Right," Megan said to her dad, "and we run the hamster through the maze, from room to room."

"Hamster? What hamster?" asked David. He looked down the table at Lainee. "Nobody ever tells me anything."

"That hamster," said Megan, pointing to the hamster cage on the floor in the corner of the dining room. "His name is Zippity."

"He belongs to the school," Lainee announced with assurance.

Zippity was awake now—go figure—and taking a rather lazy trot on the rodent wheel.

"What's a hamster doing in the dining room?" asked David.

"Aaaahhh-choo!" said Matt.

"It's only temporary," said Lainee.

"We have to return Zippity to school on Monday," said Megan. "So it's really important that we run him through the maze tomorrow."

"'We?' Who's 'we'?" asked David. "Lainee, would you pass the garlic bread, please?"

"Me and the difficult girl, Dad," said Megan.

"I don't think you should call her the 'difficult girl,'" said David.

"Mom met her," Megan protested. "Mom, tell Dad that it's true. Alexis is difficult!"

"I wouldn't say 'difficult' necessarily," said Lainee as she handed the basket of garlic bread down the table.

But just as the basket passed in front of Matt—"Aaaahhh-choo!"

Matt sneezed again, all over the garlic bread.

"*Ick,*" said Megan, as her dad set the basket aside.

"I think you're definitely coming down with something," Lainee said to Matt.

"Something disgusting," said Megan.

"Megan, leave your brother alone," said Lainee. She got up from her chair and stepped behind Matt so that she could place her hand on his forehead. "You don't feel warm," she said.

"What's that on your neck?" asked Megan. She was pointing at Matt.

Matt tilted his head to one side and both his parents gasped. Tiny red welts dotted one side of his neck.

"What is it?" said Matt.

"I think it's hives," said Lainee. "Pull up your shirt." She was already tugging on his T-shirt.

"Mom!" Matt protested.

"Don't 'Mom!' me," said Lainee. "I used to undress you all the time when you were a baby."

Matt rose from his chair and held out his hands to keep his mother back. "Mom, I'll do it *myself*, okay?"

Lainee backed off and crossed her arms. Matt lifted his T-shirt and turned around to display his bare back.

Everyone gasped. Megan dropped her fork. Her mouth hung open even though it was full of spaghetti.

"What?" Matt asked, looking over his shoulder.

His back was covered with a crazy pattern of red splotches.

"Disgusting!" said Megan.

"Megan, shush," said her mother, resting her hands comfortingly on Matt's shoulders.

"What is it?" said Matt with annoyance. He craned his neck from side to side, trying to peer at his own back.

"Trust me, you don't want to know," said Megan, with a mouthful of food.

"You've got a rash," said David. "Well, worse than a rash. It's like welts. All over your back."

"It looks like one of those connect-the-dots games," said Megan.

"Mom, make her cut it out," said Matt.

"Megan, shush," her mother repeated as she leaned closer for a better look at Matt's back.

"He asked me what it looked like, so I told him," said Megan. "Doesn't it itch? I bet it itches. If my back looked like that, I'd be itching like crazy."

"Megan, *shush!*" Lainee and David said in unison.

David rose from his chair and circled the table to examine Matt's back as well. "He must be allergic to something," David continued.

"Not garlic bread and pasta," said Lainee. "We've had garlic bread and tomato sauce and pasta before."

"Maybe it's the hamster," said David.

There was a pause in the room as everyone turned to look at the hamster cage. Zippity had given up on the rodent wheel and had curled back up into a ball.

"Zippity didn't do anything," said Megan.

"He doesn't have to," said David, "if Matt is allergic."

"We've never had a hamster in the house before," observed Lainee, stroking Matt's hair. "Were you playing with the hamster before dinner?"

"I took him out of his cage," said Matt.

"Don't touch my hamster!" Megan protested.

"Megan, please," said Lainee.

"I get in trouble if anything happens to that hamster!" Megan continued.

"I only had him out for a second," said Matt. "I let him crawl across my shoulders and under my shirt, but his little feet tickled so I put him away."

"Did he crawl across your neck and down your back?" asked Lainee.

"I think so," said Matt. "I don't remember."

"Have you ever been allergic to hamsters before?" asked David. "Maybe at school?"

"I don't think so," said Matt. "Aaaahhh-choo!"

Megan's mom and dad glanced at each other. David pointed his fork at the hamster cage.

"Oh, dear," said Lainee.

"Zippity has got to go," said David.

"No!" Megan protested. "My whole science fair project depends on Zippity!"

"But it's not fair to your brother to make him sick the weekend of his baseball tryouts!" said Lainee. "Go upstairs, Matt, and take a long, hot shower. That should take care of the hives. Then stay in your room and close the door. Go straight to bed. We're putting you in quarantine. I'll move Zippity to the garage and vacuum in here, but you should probably stay clear of the rest of the house until you feel better."

"All right," said Matt, sounding worse by the minute.

Megan felt bad for Matt. But she also felt bad for Zippity.

"We can't put Zippity in the garage all night," she argued. "How would you like it? Spending the night in the garage."

Megan's father had already left the table to pick up the hamster cage. "Zippity can file a complaint in the morning," he said.

"But what about this weekend?" Megan complained. "Without Zippity I've got no science fair project!"

"We'll call Alexis," said Lainee. "Maybe Zippity can bunk there for the weekend."

Megan wanted to protest, but she couldn't think of a comeback. Sometimes her mom had all the answers.

The next morning Megan's mom telephoned Alexis's mom. "Hello?" she said into the telephone. "Is this Alexis's mom? This is Megan's mom, Lainee Merrill. Yes! Our girls are working on a hamster maze experiment together."

Megan didn't know why her mother found the expression "hamster maze experiment" so funny.

"Is Alexis there?" Lainee asked.

Alexis's mom must have been talking for a

few moments, because Lainee said nothing. Then she said, "Oh." It wasn't encouraging.

"Where is she?" Megan asked with annoyance.

"At the library," signed Lainee.

"Probably scrounging around for extra credit," Megan signed back.

Lainee twisted her face into a warning, as though she'd scold Megan if she could. "Unfortunately, it's the hamster," she said to Alexis's mom. "My son, Matt, is allergic and we didn't know in advance because—well, we'd never had a hamster to dinner before." Megan's mom and Alexis's mom shared a little mom-laugh, and then Lainee continued. "Oh, really? You mean it?" she said into the telephone. "You wouldn't mind?"

Megan gestured "What?" but her mom wouldn't answer. She grabbed a notepad and quickly jotted down an address.

"Thank you. Thank you so much," Lainee said into the receiver. "Megan and her father will be right over with Zippity." Then she hung up the phone.

"What's up?" asked Megan.

"Grab Zippity and his cage out of the garage," said Lainee. "And find your father and find my car keys. You're dropping Zippity off with Alexis's mom."

"And the maze!" cried Megan. "I'm not moving Zippity unless we keep him with the maze."

"And the maze," repeated Lainee.

"I know this neighborhood," said Megan's dad as they turned down Beckwith Street, the street where Alexis lived. "Your mother and I once looked at a house in this neighborhood."

"The address is 587 Beckwith," said Megan, reading off the note her mother had given her. It was a pleasant two-story house, green stucco with black shutters and trim. A large Japanese maple tree filled the front yard.

"You could convince me to live here," David said, appraisingly.

"Give me a minute, Dad," said Megan. "I should be right back."

"Okeydokey," he said, parking the car along the curb.

Megan climbed out of the car, hauled the

maze out of the backseat, and carried it to the front door where she propped it against a potted plant. Then she hurried to the car for Zippity's cage, ran back to the front door, and rang the bell.

The first thing Megan noticed at the front door was that Alexis's mom was *nice*. She wore her hair braided in a thick French braid, and she answered the door in an apron dappled with flour.

The next thing Megan noticed was the smell of cinnamon.

"You're making cinnamon buns," Megan declared.

"Cinnamon, yes!" Alexis's mom cried. "I'm so embarrassed. You caught me up to my elbows in flour!" She wiped her hands off on the apron and tugged wisps of hair away from her face. Then she gazed at the girl on the doorstep, somewhat perplexed. "How did you know I was making cinnamon buns?"

"I can smell it," said Megan. "I'm Megan." She reached out to shake hands but ended up waving instead because Alexis's mom's hands were covered in flour.

"Oh, yes," said Alexis's mom. Her voice got louder as she connected Megan to her recent telephone conversation with Megan's mom and remembered that Megan was deaf. "Megan! I'm so happy to meet you!"

"I'm wearing a hearing aid," said Megan. "So you don't have to shout!"

Alexis's mom appeared confused. "Oh!" she said. "Alexis told me you were deaf but she didn't tell me—"

"I wear a hearing aid and I read lips," said Megan. "So I can understand when you talk to me, but the thing is—I can only read lips so fast. So you can talk quieter and you can slow down." Megan was accustomed to giving grown-ups and new kids the lowdown on being deaf. Megan was diagnosed as profoundly deaf, which meant she had some hearing in extremely high or low frequencies but at a very low volume or distorted and garbled.

Megan's hearing aid helped to clean up the sounds she could already barely hear—but it was more a matter of being trained to identify sounds rather than the ease of hearing most people have.

"Well, I'll talk slower then," said Alexis's mom, loudly and quickly. "Ohmigosh! That's what I'll do," she repeated, only more softly and slowly. She gestured for Megan to step inside. "Alexis is at the library, but I'll take Zippity off your hands."

Megan held on to the cage. "It's only because my brother is allergic," she said.

"Yes!" said Alexis's mom. "Your mother told me."

The third thing that Megan noticed was that Alexis's house wasn't upside-down at all. It was organized and nicely decorated. Megan was surprised that she didn't notice any moving boxes at all. "I thought you were still moving in," said Megan.

"Oh, no," said Alexis's mom. "The first thing I like to do is unpack everything! I can't stand living in a house surrounded by cardboard boxes and suitcases and all the bundles of whatever when you move."

That's strange, thought Megan. *Alexis said her house was upside-down with moving boxes. Why would Alexis lie about that?* She didn't mention anything to Alexis's mom. Instead she asked,

"Where do you want me to put Zippity?" She raised the hamster cage slightly. "I left his maze outside."

"Where to put Zippity? Where to put Zippity?" Alexis's mom repeated as though she hadn't planned on choosing the right spot for the hamster when she agreed to let Megan and Zippity come over. "I'm going to say— the coffee table in the den." She pointed through an archway.

Megan took two steps into the den and placed the cage on the small black coffee table. She turned back to Mrs. Powell and asked, "You don't have any cats, do you?"

"Cats? No," said Alexis's mom. "No, no, no."

At that moment Alexis's little brother, Justin, came barreling into the den. He bounced like a pinball off the sofa and pried his way between his mother's legs. Tumbling across the room, he rebounded off Megan and eventually collided with the small black coffee table. Stopping there for a breather, he ran his hand across one side of the hamster cage, apparently trying to pet Zippity.

"You probably shouldn't try to pet him,"

said Megan. "You've got little fingers and he might try to bite."

"You can talk to Justin but he probably won't talk back," said Alexis's mom, patting Justin's head.

"He won't talk to me?" Megan asked.

"Probably not," said Alexis's mom.

The boy's as bad as his sister, thought Megan. *Alexis won't talk to me. Justin won't talk to me. The only one in this whole family who talks to me is the mom!*

"Justin is *autistic*," Alexis's mom explained, "which means, in Justin's case, that he has difficulty talking."

Megan was puzzled. She thought she'd seen Justin talking. "You mean, he can't talk *at all*?" she asked.

"Well, he doesn't talk to *us*," Alexis's mom stated. "Autistic kids like Justin see the world differently than we do, and that complicates things like, well, communication for one. It's hard for us to understand him and it's hard for him to understand us."

"It's like that for me sometimes," said Megan. "A lot of the time. Most of the time."

"I understand you just fine," Alexis's mom said, encouragingly.

"That's not what I mean," said Megan. "I mean when people meet me, they think I can't talk at all. Then they find out—I never shut up."

Megan laughed. And Alexis's mom laughed too.

"Maybe Justin talks all the time," Megan continued, "and you don't understand."

"I bet you're right," said Alexis's mom. "I'll have to ask Justin's teachers."

"Justin goes to school?" asked Megan.

"Justin goes to a special school where the teachers can meet his special needs," Alexis's mom explained.

In the short time they had been talking, Justin had dropped his interest in Zippity and run to press his face against the sliding glass doors that opened onto the backyard. He left sticky fingerprints on the glass. Then he ran to the piano and pounded nonsensically on the keys.

"Justin, we can find another time to play the piano," said Alexis's mom. She didn't seem upset at all. She seemed perfectly accustomed to the degree of chaos that Justin brought to the house. She moved swiftly to the piano and placed her hands on top of Justin's hands. Justin stopped pounding the keys. A moment later he had turned his attention back to Zippity. He slipped away from his mother's grasp and ran to the table. He tapped on the top of the cage, trying to wake up the hamster.

It happened two or three times like that. Justin charging across the room, distracted by any number of things—and then returning to focus on Zippity in the hamster cage.

"Hamster," said Megan. She pointed at the sleeping fur ball and nodded at Justin. *"Hamster,"* she repeated, adding the sign language for the word as well. She brushed her index finger across the tip of her nose— almost as if to suggest whiskers.

"We're not sure whether Justin has any words yet," said Alexis's mom. "We think he understands words, but he has difficulty expressing himself."

Megan repeated the sign for "hamster," but

she didn't say the word out loud. Justin continued to watch her very carefully, and then abruptly turned on his heels to run in the other direction.

Megan shifted toward Alexis's mom and offered a small smile. "He really is very cute," she said, pointing at the rambunctious child.

At that moment Alexis walked through the front door with a hefty stack of library books. "Alexis!" cried her mom. "Perfect timing. Your friend Megan just arrived with Zippity, the hamster."

Alexis stopped in her tracks. She looked at Megan with an unwelcome scowl. "I saw the maze outside," she said. "What are you doing here?"

Megan was surprised at the lack of hospitality she received from Alexis. "My brother Matt—you met Matt—is allergic to hamsters," she said. "Sneezing, welts, hives, the works!"

"Megan's brother is allergic to hamsters, Alexis," Alexis's mom repeated, "so I said Zippity could spend the weekend here."

"You didn't have to let her inside!" cried

Alexis, pointing at Megan. "Couldn't you take the cage at the door? Did you have to let Megan inside?"

Megan and Alexis's mom were both taken aback by Alexis's outburst. Before either of them could say anything, Justin charged into the front hall from the den. He knocked into Alexis, tugging on her belt loops and her backpack and sending her library books crashing to the floor. He appeared to be screaming about something, but it wasn't a high-pitched scream. It was like a loud, low-pitched, thundering groan. He stomped his feet in a circle around Alexis—and then, just as abruptly, Justin returned to Zippity in the den and gently strummed his fingers across the top of the cage.

"Mom, make him stop!" shouted Alexis. "I wish he would stop it!"

"He's just being nice to the hamster," Megan said in defense of the boy. Justin seemed a little erratic, and rambunctious maybe, but he didn't seem like a bad kid. "You should show Justin how Zippity runs through the maze," Megan suggested, trying to make things better for Alexis. "I think he'd like that, don't you?

Watching the hamster run through our maze?"

"No, I don't!" snapped Alexis.

Megan backed off. She knew better than to try to talk sense to any kid who was in the middle of having a tantrum. Still, she had to say something.

"Right," said Megan. "It's not a good time for me, either. My dad is waiting in the driveway. You probably saw him sitting in the car. But before I go we should decide when we want to run the experiment. It's already Saturday and we only have until Monday to find out if Zippity likes the purple over the red and the blue."

Alexis had thrown herself onto the sofa in a serious sulk. Her arms were wrapped around a pillow that she clutched to her chest, and she refused to look at anyone. "I don't care about the purple," Alexis shouted into the pillow. "I don't care about science! I don't care about the science fair!"

"Maybe it's a bad time, Megan," suggested Alexis's mother. "Maybe you can come over tomorrow and run the hamster through the maze."

"Maybe," said Megan, although at the

moment it didn't seem very likely at all. Justin was raising a ruckus and Alexis was throwing a tantrum—and Megan certainly knew when she wasn't welcome.

She walked to the door and nodded slightly at Mrs. Powell as a way of saying so long. She flipped her hand toward both Alexis and Justin as a simple wave good-bye. Then Megan headed outside.

"Alexis wasn't there when I got there but then she came home and totally freaked out!" Megan explained to her dad in the car.

"What do you mean, 'freaked out'?" asked her father.

"She freaked out!" Megan insisted. "Screaming and yelling and crying. I didn't have anything to do with it."

"You didn't do anything to upset her?"

"Dad," Megan began, as though the idea were simply preposterous, "I was only playing with her kid brother—who's nice but a little weird—and Alexis walked in and—"

"What do you mean 'nice but weird'?" asked her dad.

"He's just weird, Dad," Megan repeated.

"I don't like that word," said David. "People aren't weird. People are different."

"Okay, okay," Megan said impatiently. "He's different, Dad."

"Say it like you mean it," said David. He continued to gaze down his nose at Megan until she felt obliged to repeat her father's saying in a more even tone of voice. "Okay, you win!" said Megan. "'People aren't weird. People are different.'"

"And how is he different?" asked David.

"He's *ausisitic*?" said Megan, trying to remember the word that Alexis's mom had used. She tried to spell it with the manual alphabet but soon gave up. "I don't know how you spell it," she said, "but that's what Mrs. Powell said about Justin. She said he's ausisisistic."

"You mean *autistic*?" asked David.

"Autistic!" Megan repeated triumphantly. "That's what he is!"

"Ohhhhhh," said Megan's dad, taking a new handle on the whole situation. "Autistic." He spelled the word correctly in the manual alphabet for Megan. It was a common routine for them. Whenever Megan encountered a new word, her dad carefully spelled out the letters with his hand—and Megan had to spell it back. As Megan grew older, the words got more and more complicated.

Reaching into her dad's line of vision, Megan carefully repeated the spelling back to him. "Okay already, 'autistic,'" she said as she finished the s-t-i-c. "What about it? What is it? What?"

"What do I look like? An encyclopedia?" asked David. He put the car into gear and headed down the street. "Look it up on the Internet."

"Okay, I will!" Megan snapped with an air of defiance. Then she laughed at her father. "You don't know what 'autistic' is either. Do you?"

"I know what it is *basically*, but not well enough to offer a good explanation," said David. "So if you find a good explanation on the Internet, I want you to share it with me."

Megan looked down her nose at her father and twisted her lips as if to say, "I told you so."

"At least I can spell it," he protested.

"All I know is," said Megan as she settled into the car seat, "whatever 'autistic' is, Alexis doesn't like it. It makes her freak out!"

Megan's father changed his grip on the steering wheel before he spoke. "Pumpkin," he began, measuring his words, "sometimes when families have kids with special needs, the special kid puts a certain strain on the moms or dads or brothers and sisters in the family."

"I don't understand," said Megan. She had no idea what her father was talking about and she wasn't afraid to say so. "I don't get it."

"It's like this," said her father, trying again. "Maybe your friend Alexis—"

"She's not my friend," interrupted Megan.

"She's the one who's practically perfect, right?"

"She's the one," said Megan.

"It sounds like Alexis likes things to be perfect," her father continued, "and she doesn't like it when they're *not*. So maybe she has to be perfect not only for herself but also for her little brother, who is maybe not so perfect because he's autistic."

"Oh," said Megan.

"And maybe Alexis doesn't want other kids to visit her at home," said Megan's dad, "because she doesn't want anyone to see her as anything *less* than perfect. Maybe she thinks her brother's autism makes her a little less perfect just because he's around."

Megan was quiet for a moment. When she finally spoke, she said, "Well, that's kind of sad."

"Yes it is," said her dad. "But it happens."

Megan fell quiet again. Then she asked, "Does being deaf make *me* less than perfect?"

Her dad knew where Megan was headed with her question, but he jumped on it. "Don't even go there," he said to Megan. "You're *you*. And we wouldn't want you to be anyone else. We don't want you to be perfect. We just want you to be *you*. Being deaf is just one of the many things you are. And in some ways being deaf makes you precisely as special as you are."

Megan mulled that thought for a moment. Then she spoke. "Okay, and Matt's my brother, right?"

"Obviously," said Megan's dad.

"Okay," said Megan, working through the formula in her mind. "So does Matt try twice as hard to be perfect because he maybe thinks that *I'm* less than perfect?"

Her dad chuckled slightly and beat the steering wheel with the palms of his hands. "Matt?" he began. "I wouldn't call Matt 'perfect.' Perfect isn't such a problem in the Merrill family."

"Matt? Perfect?" Megan laughed. She rolled happily against the car seat. "Fat chance!"

9

E-mail Me

MEGAN TYPED "AUTISTIC" INTO THE SEARCH engine.

The computer thought for a second, and then the screen displayed an orderly list of about a bazillion Web sites. Most of them looked terribly official. Some of them weren't even in English.

"Oh, brother," Megan said to herself. "I want an explanation. Not an encyclopedia!"

Megan was alone in the kitchen, perched on a chair in front of the family computer in the alcove. She wiggled the mouse to get the cursor back into the search engine box and reconsidered her search word.

All I want is a site that explains autism to a kid, she thought. *That shouldn't be so hard!* Megan blinked once or twice as she pondered the problem, and then she had a terrific idea. She set her fingers on the keyboard and typed "explain autism to a kid."

She clicked the mouse again and waited for the results.

This time a much more manageable list of Web sites popped up on the screen. Megan thought one of the listings looked friendlier than the others, because it used the word "kid" several times in the description. Megan fidgeted with the cursor and clicked on the listing. When the Web site opened, Megan was pleased to see that it contained exactly what she wanted. It had photographs of happy people, both grown-ups and kids. Bright-colored boxes contained snippets of information written in words that Megan could understand. She clicked on a box marked simply: WHAT IS AUTISM?

Autistic kids experience the world differently than most kids do.

One reason is because autistic kids react in unusual ways. For example, ordinary sounds might bother them a lot. Simple, gentle touch may feel awkward or uncomfortable.

Another reason is because autistic kids have trouble making connections. Most kids understand that a smiley face is happy or friendly. Autistic kids might not connect a smile with happy feelings. This same confusion can apply to words.

Autistic kids might not connect words with the correct meanings or with any meaning at all. They might know the word "blue" but not relate it to the color blue. As a result, autistic kids can become frustrated by words—and doubly frustrated when they try and fail to come up with the right word to express a thought or feeling.

Many autistic kids need special help in order to communicate.

Megan clicked on the icon to print the page so that she could share this information with her father. The printer jiggled slightly as the paper began to emerge. Megan rapped her fingers lightly against the keyboard. She was glad to know more about autism. Even so, knowing more about Justin's condition and the situation with Alexis's family still didn't explain why Alexis had such a problem with Megan being deaf.

What would Lizzie do? thought Megan. Lizzie was a deaf girl that Megan and Cindy had met at camp the summer before. Megan and Lizzie had spent only a few weeks together, but they had become fast friends in a short amount of time. Megan thought Lizzie was amazing. She was impressed by the way Lizzie could handle herself in any situation. And it was good to have a deaf friend who understood exactly what Megan was going through.

Unfortunately, Lizzie lived an hour away. They had promised to stay friends at the end of camp, but an hour away was too far to visit. Since they were both deaf, obviously they couldn't talk on the telephone. They had swapped e-mail addresses and screen names so that they could exchange e-mails and send instant messages to each other. Over the holidays, however, Lizzie had contacted Megan using a whole new method of communication.

Megan clicked on the icon to open a window in her instant-messaging program. She clicked on the rubber-duckie icon that was connected to Lizzie's screen name. Then she clicked on a camera icon at the upper corner of the box.

A tiny hourglass appeared on the screen. It teetered back and forth, marking the seconds as the computer tried to access Lizzie's e-mail account through the video instant-message window. Megan checked the tiny camera perched on top of her own monitor to make sure it was operating. Green light, go. Everything appeared to be working okay. She pursed her lips and blew on the keyboard to clear away a few persnickety specks of purple glitter she found there.

In a moment another window opened. It was blank at present, but in the upper corner there was a smaller box and Megan could see her own image in it. She waved into the camera on top of the computer—and waved back at herself from the computer screen.

The window went blank for an instant, and when it popped back on, Lizzie's image filled the small frame. She was smiling broadly and waving both hands in a big "Hello!" It was like talking to a friend through the television set. Megan waved back even more wildly, and the competition built until both girls went a little crazy with their hands, celebrating their reunion.

When Megan and Lizzie had first communicated this way, they'd spent most of the conversation discussing how cool the video instant-message system was. Now that the system was more familiar, the two dove into gabbing like girlfriends.

"Hey girl, what's up?" said Lizzie.

"Ohmigosh, Lizzie," Megan signed. "It is so annoying. Have you ever had a girl ignore you just because you're deaf?"

"Hello?" said Lizzie. "It happens all the time."

"But I mean, more than ignore you," Megan responded. "Have you ever had a girl be *really mean* to you just because you're deaf?"

Megan watched the screen for Lizzie's response.

Lizzie jumped in her seat and clenched her fists like a prizefighter. "Who was mean to you?" she answered. She bobbed from side to side, pretending to be a boxer.

"It's this girl, Alexis," said Megan. "But it's not like we actually fight. She's just really mean to me because I'm deaf."

"Maybe it's not because you're deaf," said Lizzie. "Maybe she just doesn't like *you*."

"That's what Matt says," Megan replied. "But I just found out that she also doesn't like me because I know her brother's autistic." She spelled the word carefully using the manual alphabet. "Do you know what that means?"

"Autistic?" Lizzie repeated. "Is that when a kid has trouble communicating? Or is that something that happens to a kid in a wheel-chair?"

"It's the communication thing," said Megan.

"That's what I thought," said Lizzie.

"There's an autistic girl at my school, but I don't know her that well. But what does this girl's autistic brother have to do with anything?"

"Maybe she's embarrassed by him and she thinks I'm going to tell people."

"*Did* you tell people?"

"Only my dad," said Megan. "And now you. It's not like it's a big deal. He's autistic. Whatever."

"Maybe it's a big deal to her," said Lizzie.

Megan flopped against her desk as though she couldn't stand another word. She pounded her fists against the top of the desk in a big dramatic display of frustration. When Megan looked up at the screen, Lizzie was laughing even as she signed, "I'm serious!"

"My sister used to have huge problems with me being deaf," said Lizzie. "She was always trying to be extra-special perfect to make up for the fact that she thought I was broken or something."

"Just like Alexis!" said Megan. "She's one of those girls that everybody thinks is so perfect. Actually, she is kind of perfect. She's smart and athletic and pretty and—"

"If she's that perfect," Lizzie interrupted, "she should figure out how incredible you are."

Megan and Lizzie shared a good laugh over that one.

"So maybe her problem is that she has to be double-perfect because she thinks her brother is less than perfect," Lizzie explained.

"That's what my dad says," said Megan. "But that's so weird."

"It happens," said Lizzie. "Happens all the time. It happened to my sister and me."

"So why does she have a problem with me?" asked Megan. "I'm not her autistic brother. I'm just this kid at school."

"Maybe you prove her wrong," said Lizzie. "'Cause you're different and you don't have a problem with it."

"You think so?" asked Megan.

"I don't know," said Lizzie. "I don't know the girl. *Ask her*. She's *your* friend."

Megan wrinkled her nose at the suggestion. "She's not my friend!" she snapped. "She's only my science fair partner."

"Oh, no!" cried Lizzie. "That's so much

worse!" She waved her hands in mock alarm. "A mean science fair partner! I wouldn't want to be in your shoes for anything in the world!"

Megan was laughing too hard to respond.

"What's your science fair project?" Lizzie asked. "Do you rub gum in her hair and see how mad she gets? Do you sneak under her desk and tie her shoelaces together and see if she falls over when she tries to stand up?"

"It's not like that!" said Megan. "We're running a hamster through a maze to see if the hamster chooses the purple room over the red room or the blue room."

This time Lizzie was laughing so hard she couldn't sign back.

"What's so funny?" asked Megan.

"That poor hamster!" said Lizzie. Megan and Lizzie both shared a good laugh.

"I'm not talking to you anymore," said Megan, catching her breath. "See you later?"

"Later," signed Lizzie.

Megan clicked on the window to close her conversation with Lizzie. Then she pivoted in her chair and began digging through zipper pockets on her backpack.

Nothing, she thought when she came up empty-handed. She poked through her notebooks and thumbed through the pages of her social studies book. *Still nothing.*

Where is it? Megan asked herself.

She checked the pockets of her warm-up jacket and double-checked her change purse. She even felt around inside her sneakers. It was only when Megan happened to look inside her own purple pencil pouch that she stumbled upon the small slip of paper with Alexis's e-mail address written on it.

Score, thought Megan.

She pivoted back to the keyboard and clicked on the mouse to open a window and compose a new e-mail.

Hey Alexis:

First off, I'm sorry things got crazy at your house this afternoon. I didn't mean to upset you and—I just didn't mean for that to happen. I only meant to drop off Zippity because he makes my brother sneeze. (Hey, maybe we should change the hamster's name to Sneeze! What do you think?)

I also want to tell you that I really like your little brother. Your mom told me how he's different and all. And I am sure he's probably a huge pain sometimes. (I know my brother can be a pain.) But I'm a little less than perfect myself, so I "get" Justin. Tell him "hey" for me.

Does this make any sense?

All for now—your friend—MEGAN

P.S. What's up with the science fair? I still want to do it. Just a question. No big deal. E-mail me back, okay?

Megan hit send.

Immediately she wished that she hadn't pushed send yet. She worried that what she had written sounded dumb or foolish, or that she had said too much when she should have said too little.

But what was the point? She'd sent it now. Alexis would either read the e-mail and like it or read it and not like it at all. It was out of Megan's control.

Except Megan had asked Alexis to e-mail her back. Megan wondered how long she should wait for a response. On heavy homework nights it was easy to get an instant reply from any friend you e-mailed because almost everyone was at the computer. However, Megan had never e-mailed Alexis before, so she didn't know how much time it might take.

Megan updated her e-mail address book and checked the in-box again. Nothing. She deleted some old mail and checked the in-box again. Still nothing. She played a quick game of computer solitaire and checked her in-box one last time. Nothing!

This is ridiculous, Megan thought. *I should give up.* She was about to shut the computer down when a small box popped open on the screen. It read: "You've got mail." Megan clicked the mouse to reveal the message, and sure enough, it was from Alexis.

Megan:
If you still want to come over and run our experiment with the hamster maze, I'm here.
Alexis

That was all. No apology. No explanation. No nothing.

Megan wasn't sure what to make of that

response. Alexis could have apologized. Alexis could have said, "Megan, you're absolutely right, and I'm totally *wrong*!" Alexis could have said, "Megan, I want you to be my friend and I will do anything to make this up to you." But all Alexis wanted was for Megan to show up so they could do the stupid hamster maze!

Megan wasn't so sure she wanted to go over there at all. That Alexis girl was too much work. She was too mean! Too perfect! Too difficult! Alexis couldn't even admit she had a problem. She was that stuck up! That worried about looking perfect all the time!

Megan had given Alexis second chance after second chance. Megan didn't think she had any second chances left in her!

At the same time, Megan had promised Mr. Ryan, Ms. Endee, *and* Jann that she and Alexis would work together on the science fair project. This weekend was the only chance to make that happen. And it sounded like Alexis wanted to make that happen too. It wasn't necessarily a matter of helping Alexis pretend to be perfect. It was a matter of Megan meeting her own commitments.

If only Matt hadn't been allergic to Zippity so they could have run the hamster maze at Megan's house instead. Then Megan would never have had to go to Alexis's house in the first place. The last thing she wanted to do was go back to Alexis's now.

At that moment, Matt descended the back stairs into the kitchen, dropping his baseball gear all over the floor. He was frantic and his hair looked like he had just rolled out of bed. "I'm gonna be late for baseball tryouts!" he shouted.

"Are you feeling better?" Megan asked. "Are you still sneezing? Are your gross hives gone?"

"Why didn't anybody wake me?" Matt groused. Apparently he was back to his old self.

"I woke you an hour ago," said Megan's dad, who had followed Matt down the back stairs, "but you fell back to sleep. I guess you needed the rest."

"But I said wake me on *time*," said Matt. "Now I'm gonna be late."

"Don't look at *me*," said Megan. "I got up early to save your life by taking Zippity over to Alexis's house, only to get yelled at by Alexis because I was playing with her little brother."

"What?" asked Matt. The expression on his face indicated that he didn't want to know the whole story. He simply didn't think Megan was making sense.

"That's not exactly what happened," said Megan's dad, reaching for the car keys on the hook. "I'll go warm up the car," he said to Matt, "so I'll be in the driveway when you're ready."

"So what happened?" said Matt, hurriedly tying the laces on his baseball shoes.

"Alexis has a kid brother who's autistic," Megan explained. "So he looks normal but he's not."

"I know what autistic means. It means he's normal but he's got a problem," Matt said, correcting her. "Being autistic is just a problem."

"Right, right, right, whatever," said Megan. "So anyway, Alexis walked in and freaked out because I was playing with her autistic brother, and Dad says it's because Alexis has to be perfect all the time."

"I gotta go," said Matt, grabbing his baseball glove and his batting helmet.

"But, Matt," said Megan, "now Alexis wants me to go over there and do our science fair experiment, but I don't want to go."

Matt hesitated. "Don't you want to see how Zippity handles the maze?" he asked. "Don't you want to know whether Zippity chooses purple? Don't you want to be in the science fair?"

"Of course I do," Megan said begrudgingly.

"Then get in the car," said Matt. "We'll drop you off at Alexis's house on the way."

"But Matt—," Megan protested.

"Hurry!" Matt demanded. "I'm already late for tryouts!"

10

Lost and Found

MEGAN'S DAD INSISTED ON WAITING AT THE curb until Megan signaled him that somebody had opened the door at Alexis's house. It was Alexis herself who opened the door. There was a slight moment of awkwardness between them but before anyone said anything, Megan motioned "One second!" She leaped off the front step onto the walkway where she waved her arms overhead, signaling her dad that he could pull away from the curb and get Matt to baseball tryouts. Matt was leaning out the car window, doing sign language for "Good luck!" Megan signed "Good luck!" back at him. Alexis was still holding the door open. "I'm sorry about what happened," she said with a bashful wince.

"Forget about it," said Megan. "I already did." Of course, she hadn't forgotten at all. She only said that so they could get on with the hamster experiment. Alexis headed inside and Megan followed.

"I asked Mom to make Justin take his nap so that he won't bug us when we run Zippity through the maze," said Alexis.

"You don't think he'd want to watch?" said Megan. "He seemed to really like that hamster."

"Trust me," said Alexis. "We don't want him in our hair. He's a total pest. If we let him run loose around that hamster, it will be a total disaster."

"I think your little brother is cute," said Megan.

Alexis scrunched her face. "Cute? He's not cute."

"Alexis, he's cute," Megan insisted. "He's got that curly hair, and he's kind of cuddly, and he runs around all the time like somebody let a teddy bear loose." Megan snickered, recalling the way Justin collided into everything in the room.

"You don't have to live with him all the time," said Alexis. "It's a real challenge, believe me. You don't know."

"You're right," Megan agreed. "But I live with being deaf. That's a challenge too."

Alexis hesitated slightly. Then she said, "I don't want to talk about this right now. Maybe we should do the hamster maze."

"Whatever," said Megan with a flip of her hand. Alexis led Megan through the kitchen and into the laundry room, where the maze had been stacked on top of the washing machine. Working together, the girls lifted it down and carried it toward the kitchen table. As they did, Alexis asked, "Can't they fix it?"

"Fix what?"

"Your hearing," said Alexis.

"They can't fix my hearing," said Megan with a little laugh. "I'm deaf."

"But can't they fix your ears?" asked Alexis.

"My ears aren't broken," said Megan. "They

don't work. Well, they did for a while when I was really little but it's not like I remember. All I remember is being deaf. So that's me—I'm deaf. That's what I am."

"Sorry," said Alexis. "I mean I'm sorry you're deaf, and I'm sorry I said something stupid."

"Don't be sorry," said Megan. "It makes me who I am. I'm not sorry about it. What fun is that?"

Alexis eyed Megan curiously. "I guess you're right."

"I know I'm right," said Megan. "I know a little bit about being deaf."

Megan smiled and Alexis smiled too. They set the maze down on the kitchen table and adjusted the corner so that it was square. It felt like things were okay between Megan and Alexis. Megan figured she could ask a tough question of her own but she approached it carefully. "Hey, Alexis. Can I ask you a question?" she said. "You could totally have won that spelling bee, right? You're smart. You know how to spell 'perceive.' You only let Ronnie Jiu win because you didn't want to win," said Megan. "Am I right?"

"Maybe," Alexis said sheepishly.

Megan figured, under the circumstances, "maybe" was as good as "yes." "Why did you do that?"

"I didn't say I did. I only said maybe."

"Right," said Megan, unconvinced. "You want to know what I think?"

"Not really."

"I think you lost the spelling bee because you didn't want your whole family to show up at the big spelling bee finals," Megan continued.

"I don't know what you're talking about."

Megan crossed her arms and spoke her mind. "You were afraid your mom would show up at the spelling bee with your little brother, Justin, and embarrass you.

Alexis rolled her eyes like she couldn't believe her ears. "I don't know where you came up with that," she said. "I wanted to win the spelling bee. 'Perceive' is just one of those words I always mess up. Ask my mom. I came home and cried because I messed up that stupid word."

"Really?"

"I'm not a great loser," said Alexis. "My dad has this thing about—'aim for excellence'—and he gets really disappointed when I'm not the best at something."

Megan tilted her head. "My dad says there's no chance that anybody in my family is perfect."

"You're lucky," said Alexis. "My mom and dad expect me to be perfect."

Megan tilted her head to the other side. "Really?"

"It feels that way sometimes," said Alexis.

"Your mom didn't seem like that to me."

"Stick around," said Alexis. "You haven't even met my dad yet."

Megan shook her head, unconvinced. "I think you're the one who likes being perfect," she said, poking a finger at Alexis. "Perfect is easy for you."

"It's not that easy," said Alexis.

"So you admit that you're perfect?"

Alexis leaned against the table. "I think maybe we better do the hamster experiment," she said.

Megan could tell Alexis wanted to change

the subject. "Okay, sure," she agreed although neither of them budged. They stood at opposite ends of the kitchen table with the hamster maze between them. Megan's lips were pursed as though she had something on her mind. She hadn't planned on saying what she said next, but for some reason she felt like being really direct with Alexis. Megan had been totally honest when Alexis asked her about being deaf, but she didn't think Alexis had been 100 percent honest when she had asked her about losing the spelling bee. Megan felt that surprising Alexis with a hard-to-ask question might force her to be more honest—and before Megan knew it, the hard-to-ask question popped out.

"Alexis, you don't like deaf people, do you?"

Alexis looked surprised. "That's not true."

"I think it is," Megan replied. "Because of the way you acted when you first met me and—well, I still think it sometimes."

Alexis's mouth hung open for a few seconds. She couldn't think of anything to say.

"You're so mean to me all the time," Megan

continued. "It seems like you never look at me when I'm talking to you. I do nice things for you, and you never say 'thank you.' Not really."

Megan was on a roll.

"And Alexis, you don't know it," she added, "but you scrunch your nose when you talk to a person you don't like." Megan circled the table, scrunching her nose in an imitation of Alexis with an attitude.

"I do not do that!" Alexis protested. Then she shielded her nose behind her hand.

"You do it a lot," said Megan, nodding. It was just a fact.

"Do I?" asked Alexis, lowering her hand. "How can you do something and not even know about it?"

"Don't ask me," said Megan. "You're the one who does it."

"But that's so weird!"

"Not so weird," said Megan. "Besides, my dad says people aren't 'weird.' He says, 'People are different.'"

"Now I'm afraid to react to anything," said Alexis. "It's like I can't control it."

"It's okay," said Megan, tugging gently on

Alexis's arm. "I'm used to it. I already figured out that you don't like me."

"I like you fine," Alexis protested. "I like you a lot! I don't know why you think I don't!"

"You're doing that thing with your nose again," said Megan, pointing at Alexis's face. Alexis was upset and defensive, and her nose twitched like a rabbit.

Alexis gasped and turned bright red. She leaned over to the toaster to peek at her nose.

"Believe me now?" said Megan.

Alexis faced Megan. "I do like you, Megan," she said. "Maybe I was uncomfortable at first, I don't know. I was in a new school. I didn't know anybody. And I hadn't met anyone like you before."

"You never met anyone who was deaf?" asked Megan.

"I'd met deaf kids before. I'd met lots of kids who are 'different' before."

"So how come you didn't like me?" asked Megan.

"I liked you fine," Alexis insisted. "But you were so popular. And you had so many friends. I'd never met anyone like *you*."

"So how come you said no when I invited you to my party?" Megan held out a hand as though she expected Alexis to drop her answer into it.

Alexis flipped her hair out of her face and then she said, "Maybe you're right. Kids who are different make me nervous. It's like with my brother. I never know what to expect."

"But you know what to expect with *me*," said Megan. "I have always been nice to you."

"Not really," said Alexis. "You're kind of moody. Sometimes you're hard to talk to. You always have to be the center of attention. And sometimes you're friendly and other times you're judging me or waiting for me to mess up. It's like you expect me to be perfect all the time. It makes me really nervous."

That wasn't the response Megan had expected. This time it was Megan's turn to let her mouth hang open. She couldn't think of anything to say except, "Wow, I had no idea."

"It's kind of true," said Alexis.

The girls sat in silence for a moment, both deep in thought. Megan was wondering if she had a mistaken impression of Alexis—and Alexis was wondering the same thing about Megan. Megan suspected she was right about Alexis— Megan's radar went off when people were uncomfortable with deafness. *But maybe*, she thought, *maybe I should cut Alexis some slack.* Megan couldn't imagine what it would be like to have people expect you to be perfect all the time.

At the same time, Megan wondered if what Alexis said was true—about her being moody and difficult, and having to be the center of attention. Megan had so much to think about that her head was spinning.

Megan sat straight up and flapped her hands to clear the air of all these thoughts. "So, Alexis," she declared, "all I really meant to say was that—even though we don't always get along—you're still invited to my birthday party. In case you were wondering."

Alexis smiled a bit, but she didn't say yes or no. She didn't even say "Thanks." She only shrugged.

Megan shrugged too. "Yeah, so you let me know when you make up your mind whether to come to my party or not. Whatever. In the meantime we better run that hamster through our maze."

"Good idea," Alexis said, raising a hand, "but Megan, before we get started—if I ask a favor, do you promise not to get mad?"

"Why would I get mad?"

"Just promise."

"I won't get mad," said Megan, raising her own hand in the Brownie pledge. "I promise."

Alexis began shyly. "It's okay if you know about Justin and his condition," she said, "but could you keep it a secret? Just for now? I don't want all the other kids at school talking about it or asking me questions about it or whatever."

"I can keep a secret! Trust me! Your secret's safe with me!" Megan zipped her lip and threw away the imaginary key. "But Justin *is* your kid brother," she continued, "and he happens to be autistic. You can't keep it a secret for *life*."

Alexis didn't say anything.

I guess I got her, thought Megan. *She didn't have an answer for that.*

"Like, I mean," Megan went on, "my

brother doesn't ever try to keep *me* a secret."

"You? Fat chance keeping *you* a secret," Alexis said, and laughed. Her laughter caught Megan by surprise. "You're having a big birthday party, and your favorite color is purple. Your best friend is Cindy, and you're not crazy about grammar or spelling but you work real hard, and you're really good at math. *And* you're deaf. I've only known you a week and look how much I know about you."

"I know stuff about you," Megan argued back. "I know you're practically perfect, but you're really shy."

"I'm not that shy," said Alexis.

"I know that now," said Megan, "but look how hard I had to work! You should let people know you're not shy. People would like you."

Alexis was quiet for a moment. Then all she said was, "Maybe."

Megan gave Alexis a sock in the arm. "Let's go get this hamster," she said. Megan cupped her hands and called about the kitchen like she was hollering for pigs. "Wake up, Zippity! It's showtime! Where's that hamster? Where's Zippity?"

Alexis laughed at Megan's antics. "I think he's in the den," she said.

"Let's go!" cried Megan, swatting Alexis and running for the door.

The girls charged into the den, racing each other to reach the hamster cage. "First!" cried Megan when she tagged the short black table. Megan was a bit out of breath from their mad dash, and she was still laughing.

But Alexis wasn't.

"Oh, no!" she cried, peering into the cage.

"What's the matter?"

"The hamster!" Alexis said, raising the empty cage. "Zippity is gone!"

11

Say Hamster

"HE COULDN'T HAVE GONE FAR," SAID MEGAN.
"Zippity has to be here somewhere."

The girls perched on either side of the
empty cage. Zippity was definitely gone.
Megan had even stuck her hand inside the
cage to pat among the wood chips and make
sure that the hamster wasn't just hiding. All
she found was the little rubber ball that
Zippity used as a toy.

Alexis was distraught. "But what if we don't
find him? Mr. Ryan made us responsible for
his life! How are we going to explain to the

whole class that Zippity ran away while we were supposed to be watching him?"

"Maybe he didn't run away," said Megan. "Maybe your mom is playing with him."

Alexis looked doubtful. "I don't think my mom plays with hamsters," she said.

"Maybe your dad."

"My dad's away on a business trip," said Alexis. "He won't be back until Monday."

"So what about Justin?" asked Megan.

Alexis's eyes grew wide with concern. "Oh, no," she cried. "You don't think—Oh, no!— Justin!" Alexis got up from the table and paced back and forth across the den.

"Justin really liked the hamster," said Megan, trying to be helpful. "Maybe he took him out. Or maybe he accidentally let him out. Or maybe—"

"Or maybe he hurt him!" said Alexis, really upset. "Justin plays too rough! He always plays too rough! I knew it was a good idea to keep Justin out of sight! He always ruins things! Now Justin's going to be the one who hurt the hamster, and everyone in the whole school is going to know about it." She stopped in her tracks. "And the whole school's going to know about Justin!"

"It's no good freaking out about it, Alexis," said Megan. "We should concentrate on finding Zippity. If we find him and he's okay, our problem is solved."

"But how are we going to find one little fur ball in this great big house? We already know he can run and he can squeeze himself into little corners and little hiding places!"

"You're still freaking out, Alexis," said Megan, trying to stay calm herself. She tightened her lips and tried to think. "Maybe the first thing we should do is—" Megan stopped. She didn't have any idea what to do.

"The first thing is what?"

Megan pointed upstairs. "The first thing is to go to Justin's room and see if he has Zippity. They might be curled up in a ball together and everything will be all right."

The girls raced upstairs to Justin's room. Alexis didn't even bother to knock on the door. "Justin!" she cried.

But Justin's room was empty.

"I thought you said he was taking a nap," said Megan.

"He was," said Alexis. Even so, Justin's bed was empty.

Alexis walked knowingly to Justin's closet and searched inside. She appeared to know Justin's favorite hiding places. She opened the toy chest and poked among the stuffed animals. Then she got on her haunches and looked under the bed. *"Justin!"* she said, rather harshly.

Megan got down on the floor and looked under the bed as well. There, pressed against the far wall, was Justin. He was curled up in a ball, almost like the hamster. Alexis shouted, "Justin, come out here!" But Justin didn't obey. He just curled tighter and tighter in the shadows under the bed.

Megan didn't like to watch Alexis yell at her little brother. She didn't like watching Justin so scared either. She pulled herself off the floor and sat on the far edge of Justin's bed, feeling extremely out of place. She could tell from Alexis's behavior that she was shouting at Justin, but he still didn't come out from under the bed. Alexis was on the verge of tears. She stomped about the room and stormed into the hall, presumably in search of her mother.

Megan was left alone in the room with Justin. Only Justin was still hiding under the bed.

Megan noticed a rubber bike horn on the carpet in front of the bureau. Megan knew about bike horns, but she had never played with them much because she couldn't hear a thing. She knew that if you squeezed the red rubber ball on one end of the horn, it made a honking sound. She held the bike horn in her hand and honked it once. Then she did it a couple more times. She even bounced up and down on the mattress a bit, hoping to get Justin's attention.

Nothing happened.

Megan took the bike horn and held it near her heels, dangling over the side of the bed. She reached lower and honked the horn along the bedspread, here and there, like a little surprise.

After a moment Megan saw the tip of Justin's head poke out from underneath the bed. He was peeking between the fringed edges of the bedspread.

The moment she saw Justin, Megan darted across the room and crouched on the floor beside the toy chest, just like a hamster would. When Justin twisted to see where she had gone, Megan scampered across the toy chest to another corner of the room. She cupped her hands like paws and held them at her nose, the same way that Zippity always did. And she pretended to be asleep.

Peeking out of one eye, Megan saw Justin emerge from underneath the bed. He stood on his stocky little legs and took short deliberate steps until he was right beside Megan. Then he crouched beside her and began to pet Megan's head.

Megan opened her eyes slowly because she didn't want to scare the little boy. She sat back on her heels and smiled. Justin seemed to smile back.

"We can't find Zippity," Megan said. "We can't find the hamster." Justin kept smiling so Megan had no way of knowing whether he understood her or not. "We're afraid the hamster might have run away. Have you seen him?"

Justin kept smiling. He seemed to be waiting for Megan to dart to another corner of the room. "We have to return Zippity to the school on Monday, or we'll be in big trouble," Megan said. "Big trouble."

Justin didn't seem to understand a single word, and Megan knew she was getting nowhere. Then she had an idea.

"Hamster," she said, brushing her index finger across her nose—as she had earlier that day. "You remember Zippity? Remember hamster?" Megan kept repeating the word and repeating the gesture.

After a moment Justin reached up and brushed his nose with his finger as well.

"That's right!" Megan cheered, clapping her hands. "Hamster, hamster!"

Megan and Justin sat there, signing hamster back and forth, over and over.

After the eighteenth "hamster," Megan realized that she was still getting nowhere. Justin could do the gesture, but he probably didn't understand what he was saying in sign. Justin was just playing a game.

Megan patted Justin's knee. "I have to go now," she said.

Justin said "hamster" in sign.

"That's right! Hamster! Bye-bye, now! Bye-bye." Megan stood at the doorway, waving good-bye.

Justin didn't say good-bye. Instead he said "hamster" again.

Megan chuckled to herself and headed downstairs to find Alexis.

Megan found Alexis in the kitchen with her mother. "Maybe we can replace the hamster," Alexis's mom was saying. "People replace hamsters all the time. One hamster basically looks the same as another."

"But kids know Zippity!" cried Alexis. "They'd know it wasn't the same hamster!"

"And he's got a little tuft of white fur under his chin," said Megan. "Kids talk about that. They know that little tuft of fur. So we couldn't replace him unless we found a hamster with the exact same thing."

Megan couldn't believe it had come to this. Was she actually discussing substituting a different hamster for Zippity?

"I think he'll turn up," said Alexis's mother. "Hamsters are notorious for that. They run away and hibernate—and everybody panics— and then they show up in the bread box. So everybody panicked over nothing."

Alexis looked inside the bread box. "He's not there," she said.

"Well, not yet, anyway," said Alexis's mother. "We'll have to keep looking."

Megan and Alexis exchanged a look. They seemed to agree that the situation was looking pretty grim for poor old Zippity.

At that moment Justin walked into the room. He teetered in the doorway and then he walked directly over to Megan. He brushed his index finger across his nose. Megan did it back. And Justin brushed his finger across his nose again.

Alexis and her mother watched in silence. When Megan returned the gesture a second time, Alexis said, "What does that mean?"

"Hamster," said Megan. "It's sign language for hamster."

Alexis and her mother looked at each other, amazed.

"I taught him earlier today and we were just practicing it upstairs," said Megan. Justin was tugging on Megan's jeans and saying "hamster" in sign at the same time. "Kind of cute, huh?"

"You don't understand," said Alexis.

"Justin has never said a word before," said Alexis's mom. Her eyes were welling slightly with tears. "Not a *spoken* word, that is. This is the first word we've ever heard him say. I mean, *seen* him say, not *heard* him say! But sign language counts!"

"His first word is hamster." Alexis chuckled, sad and happy at the same time. "Teach me," she said to Megan.

"It's easy," said Megan, brushing her finger across her nose. "Hamster."

"Hamster," repeated Alexis.

Alexis's mom signed it too. "Hamster."

Justin reached for Megan's hand and took Alexis's hand as well. Tugging both girls, Justin led them into the laundry room. As Alexis's mom watched from the kitchen, Justin got on all fours and crawled toward the back of the dryer, pointing to the vent where the warm air came out. He held himself up on one arm and brushed his nose with his hand.

"What are you trying to tell us, Justin?" said Alexis.

"He's telling us *hamster*," said Megan.

Megan and Alexis crawled over the dryer to peer into the warm gap beyond. There was Zippity, tucked among the dust bunnies. He was curled happily into a ball, with the hot air from the vent warming him.

"Mom, get the broom," cried Alexis. "We found the hamster!"

Mrs. Powell arrived with the broom, but the first thing she did was scoop Justin off the ground. "What a breakthrough!" she cheered, hugging her son and smothering his face with kisses. "Who's my talking boy? Who's my talking boy?"

Alexis was kneeling on top of the dryer. She took the broom and poked it into the space beyond. When Zippity came running around the corner of the dryer, Megan was waiting to scoop him into a laundry basket.

Alexis hopped off the dryer and brushed her knees. She and Megan exchanged a victorious smile. Alexis's mom was still dancing about the laundry room with Justin in her arms. Alexis wrapped her arms around her mother's waist and joined the dance, laughing joyfully.

Megan stood to one side with a big smile on her face and cupped Zippity tightly between the palms of her hands. She watched the Powell family do their little dance, and it felt like she had never seen anybody so happy before.

While Mrs. Powell made grilled cheese sandwiches to celebrate Justin's first word and the return of Zippity, Megan and Alexis put Zippity into the maze on top of the kitchen table.

"Please, please, don't let him get out," said Alexis's mom.

"Don't worry!" said Alexis.

"We won't," added Megan.

Megan and Alexis let Justin stand on a kitchen chair between them so that he could watch Zippity in action. They each also kept a watchful hand on his waistband to make sure he didn't fall off his chair.

The first time Zippity ran the maze, he

reached the red room and refused to budge. Megan and Alexis couldn't mask their disappointment. Alexis was keeping track of the score on a yellow pad and she drew a sad face beside the results of the first run.

"I can't believe he chose red!" Megan protested. "Red is awful!"

However, the second, third, and fourth times that Zippity ran the maze, he chose the purple room—three times in a row!

"Purple's on a winning streak," Megan crowed.

In the fifth run Zippity chose blue, but he never chose blue again after that. "Zippity must hate blue," said Alexis.

"Probably true," Megan agreed.

In the sixth run Zippity chose purple. And although he visited the red room on the eighth or ninth try, the rest of the time he always chose purple. Almost each and every time.

"Proving without a doubt," said Megan, as Alexis tallied the score, "that purple is by far the greatest color!"

"Indubitably!" said Alexis.

The girls let Justin stroke Zippity with his fingertip a few times before they tucked the hamster back into his cage.

"Zippity has earned his beauty sleep tonight," said Alexis.

"Definitely," said Megan.

They called Megan's dad from the kitchen, and—this time it was Alexis who sat with Megan on the front step, waiting for *her* dad's car to show up.

"Look," said Alexis, pointing at the night sky. "It's purple."

"The absolute greatest," said Megan.

"Without a doubt, the best," said Alexis.

"I think it's some kind of sign," said Megan. "Because you know, there's still this birthday party happening, and it's still all purple, and you know you're still invited."

Alexis smiled. But she didn't say a word.

12

Red Ribbon, Blue Ribbon

"'CHROMATIC ABERRATION AND ACHROMATIC Lenses,'" read Cindy. "I don't even know what that means!"

"Ask Alexis," said Megan.

"Hey, Alexis," Cindy shouted down Winners' Alley at the science fair. "What does 'Chromatic Aberration and Achromatic Lenses' mean?"

"Beats me," said Alexis. She walked toward them and eyeballed the exhibit. "What did it win?"

"A blue ribbon," said Megan. "First place."

The girls shook their heads, mystified by the success. "Go figure," said Cindy. Megan leaned forward to read the details about the student who had conducted the experiment. "He's in the *seventh* grade," she announced. The girls groaned as though that information explained everything.

"Seventh graders," said Alexis. "They think they're so smart."

The school science fair occupied the gymnasium. Card tables and poster-board exhibits were arranged in eight aisles across what was otherwise the basketball court. Mr. Ryan had labeled the aisles with amusing placards like WINNERS' ALLEY and THE TOP TEN COUNTDOWN.

The science fair judges included Mr. Ryan, Principal Smelter, and Tony Glenn, the weatherman from the local television station. Despite the panel's unquestionable qualifications, Megan, Alexis, and Cindy weren't convinced the judges had made the right decisions. For example, the big Grand Prize winner didn't really deserve it. "'Which Spiders Eat Other Spiders?'" said Megan. "That's just wrong!"

"If I'd been awarding the Grand Prize," Alexis declared, "I'd have given it to '"How Skin Heals."'" The exhibit contained several close-up photographs of scabs in various stages of recovery. Most of the boys flocked around the gruesome examples of "What happens when you 'pick.'" The important part of the exhibit was a series of remarkably detailed photographs following a scab through the natural healing process all the way back to healthy skin.

"Not me," said Cindy, "I'd give it to 'A Model Swamp in a Tank.'" A pair of sixth graders had recreated the Okefenokee Swamp in a fish aquarium. At first glance it looked as if the students had simply stopped cleaning the aquarium. However, the exhibit notes indicated the extensive research the students had done in order to authentically recreate a swamp. "It's really fascinating," said Cindy, "even if it is kind of stinky."

"My prize goes to 'Tap Water: Something's Swimming in the Sink,'" said Megan. The exhibit consisted of an ordinary glass of tap water and a slide show of unbelievably creepy bugs. The girls cooed in mutual appreciation, even though the exhibit was more horror movie than science fair project.

The girls continued down Winners' Alley, taking in top exhibits with less impressive titles like "If the Earth Was a Cube," "Bridges That Fall Down and Why," and "Uses of the Wedge." "Operation of a Doorbell" was interesting at first but got old real fast.

Megan's fourth-grade class claimed a spot on Winners' Alley with a rather ridiculous contribution by two burly boys named Tim and Tom. It was called "Farts: Fact or Fiction." The red ribbon on the poster meant a second-place prize. Megan said that Tim and Tom had probably been studying farts their entire lives.

"What have these exhibits got that ours hasn't got?" asked Alexis.

"I know, right?" said Megan. "Like 'Weeds near My Home.' That kid won a green ribbon—third place! And you know he pulled that exhibit together on the way to school. With his bare hands!"

The girls had a good laugh over that one.

Mr. Ryan dedicated an entire section of the

science fair to "The Volcano." Megan joked that it should have been called "A Salute to Papier-Mâché." The exhibitions ran the gamut of fake volcanoes—from chemical reactions with baking soda to basic physics involving a simple crank and puffed rice. Every five minutes a fake explosion drew a small round of applause.

"Let's head over to my exhibit," said Cindy. Cindy's experiment with Tony Rosenblum, "The Absorption Rate of Diapers," had been a surprise hit with the judges. "Mostly because of all the useful information," according to Cindy. It was marked with a yellow ribbon like all the other honorable-mention exhibits and situated in a center aisle that Mr. Ryan liked to call "Almost Won Boulevard."

The science fair was pretty terrific, but after a while the event became a little overwhelming. "You get lost in the questions," said Alexis.

"I know," said Megan. "Like, 'How Do Detergents Affect Brine Shrimp?' and 'Can Goldfish Learn?'"

The girls took a breather just across from an exhibit called "The Life Cycle of the Cockroach."

"Can you imagine?" asked Cindy, scrunching her face and shielding her eyes from the display.

"Ick. I could never," said Megan.

Cindy shifted toward Megan and Alexis. "So where are you guys?" she asked. "Where's your exhibit? What'd you win?"

Megan and Alexis exchanged a glance. They had compiled their results and put together a poster-board display with the words "Hamsters Prefer Purple" stenciled across the top.

"We didn't win a prize," Alexis admitted with a shrug.

"We're on 'Weird Science Lane,'" said Megan, pointing to the sign a few aisles down. "Only it's not 'Weird Science.' It's 'Different Science'!"

"Check it out," said Alexis, nudging Cindy. "We're right between 'Can Carnations Change Color?' and 'How High Can a Dog Count?'"

"Oh, no!" cried Cindy, trying to hide her giggles.

"Ah, well," Megan said, "we had fun with

Zippity and our hamster maze. Let's go hang out by our exhibit so we can answer people's questions."

"There you guys are," said Matt. He was showing passersby how to run Zippity through the hamster maze and answering questions from fifth-grade boys who were certain the maze was rigged. The boys were complaining, "No hamster likes purple *that much*."

"This one does," Matt responded.

Right on cue, Zippity ran nimbly through the maze and curled up in a ball once he reached the purple room.

"It's rigged!" the fifth-grade boys protested.

"Move along," said Matt, who was babysitting Zippity from behind the card table.

"We're moving," said the boys, not looking for trouble at the science fair.

"Congratulations on making the baseball team, Matt," said Cindy.

"Oh, you made the team?" said Alexis. "Congratulations!"

"Megan told me all about it!" bragged Cindy.

"Our first practice game is next weekend if you want to come," said Matt.

"We'll be there!" all three girls chimed in unison.

"Oh, great," Matt muttered. "My own personal cheerleaders."

The girls laughed and launched into an improvised cheer, chanting "Go, Matt!" over and over until it was really obnoxious.

Matt blushed slightly—and Megan beamed with pride.

Mr. Ryan approached the podium; his hair was frizzed out and he was wearing a comically thick pair of Coke-bottle glasses. He was also wearing a white laboratory coat and a pair of green rubber gloves. He tapped the microphone to make sure it was on and twisted the gooseneck so that the mike reached his mouth.

A shrill screech from the PA system got everyone's attention focused on the gymnasium stage. Most of the kids were holding their hands over their ears and begging for relief.

Jann was positioned at one side of the stage, next to the American flag, where she was ready to translate Mr. Ryan's remarks into sign language.

"My fellow scientists," Mr. Ryan said into the microphone. "As you know, we gave out the big prizes this morning. The blue ribbons, the red, the green, and the yellow. How about another round of applause for the big winners?"

Mr. Ryan stepped away from the podium and clapped his rubber gloves together like a seal. The students in the gymnasium whistled and cheered. Jann waved her hands overhead to indicate the sound of applause.

Mr. Ryan returned to the microphone. "We also awarded the special Grand Prize to Jonathan Gaines and Karen Stetson for their exhibit, 'Which Spiders Eat Other Spiders?' We are pleased to announce that this project will represent our school in the county science fair competition."

There was another mild smattering of applause. Megan made a face as though she were gagging on a spider.

At that moment Alexis spotted her mother and Justin heading down the adjoining aisle, where all the interactive exhibits were located. Interactive displays were big crowd favorites—like "Fingerprints: Only You Are You" and "Bubbles: Films and Surface Tension." Another popular exhibit was "Popcorn Popping Rates" but mostly because of the free samples. Justin barreled down the aisle, as usual. Alexis cringed in anticipation of all the toppled card tables he would leave in his wake.

"Hey, Mom," she called out. Mrs. Powell caught sight of Alexis and signaled that she would circle around and head in their direction.

"Mom's here with Justin," Alexis said to Megan, pointing at the next aisle.

"Oh, boy!" said Megan. In the days since they had successfully run the hamster maze, Megan had been over to Alexis's house twice. She'd taught Justin to say "more" in sign language—he would clench his hands into loose fists and then tap-tap-tap his fingertips together—and now it was Justin's favorite new word of the two words he knew. No matter what the subject, Justin wanted "more."

More kick-ball, more milk, more hotdog, and—his favorite use of the word—more hugs.

"Justin!" cried Megan as the boy charged down their aisle with Alexis's mom. Megan squatted low so she could catch Justin in a hug. When he landed in her arms with a plunk, Alexis reached down to gently tousle his hair.

"Cindy hasn't met Justin yet," said Megan.

"No, but I've heard a lot about him," said Cindy.

"Cindy, this is Justin," said Alexis, gesturing toward her little brother. "Justin, this is Cindy. And this is my mom, Mrs. Powell."

"Hello, Mrs. Powell."

"Nice to meet you, Cindy," said Alexis's mom.

Justin tugged away from Megan's arms to beat his hands against the edge of the card table that contained their hamster maze. Their poster-board display wobbled perilously back and forth.

"No, Justin, no!" cried Alexis.

"It's okay," said Megan. "He's trying to tell us something."

Justin was tapping his fingertips together and brushing his nose.

"He's saying 'more hamster'!" said Alexis.

"Justin put two words together!" said Megan.

"'More hamster'!" the girls cried. Mrs. Powell scooped Justin up from the ground as the girls applauded and cheered.

"Shhhhhh!" said Cindy. "Mr. Ryan is trying to present the awards!"

"Where's Mom and Dad?" Megan asked Matt. "I don't want them to miss this part!"

"They're getting fingerprinted," said Matt, jerking his thumb toward the interactive aisle. "So shhhhhhh!" He pressed a finger to his lips.

Megan hushed down and turned to face the stage.

"In addition to the big winners," Mr. Ryan was saying in a terribly serious voice, "we also select winning exhibits in the categories of silliest and goofiest, and we present the Deep Space Award for the most 'way-out' project of all." The kids issued a roar of appreciation for their favorite part of the event.

"This year the Silliest Award goes to Mickey Birnbaum and Alicia Wollerton for 'MUD: *Many Uses of Dirt*.'" A polite round of applause greeted Mickey and Alicia as they bounded for the stage to accept their award.

"The Goofiest Award," Mr. Ryan continued, "goes to TJ and Davis Ryan for 'Where Wombats Come From.'" A cheer went up among the sixth graders as TJ and Davis raced for the stage and their ribbon. They bowed and blew kisses at the crowd.

"And last but not least, the Deep Space Award for the most 'out there' project in the science fair . . . ," Mr. Ryan began. He paused slightly to build suspense, and then he continued, ". . . goes to Yolanda Vera and Martha Matthews for 'Invertebrates on Parade'!"

Mr. Ryan couldn't have known that he was presenting the Deep Space Award to the two kids at Wilmot Elementary who everybody suspected came from another galaxy. Martha and Yolanda were the kind of friends who stuck together like glue, spoke a secret language, and laughed at little jokes nobody else could understand. Name-calling wasn't allowed at Wilmot

Elementary, but more than one kid had eyed the two girls, nudged a friend, and pointed up, as if at a distant planet.

Even so, Martha and Yolanda had produced the surprise hit of the science fair. They'd constructed detailed clay replicas of invertebrates and suspended them from wires that jiggled while the girls played marching music on kazoos. It really was "Invertebrates on Parade," and the entire school was apparently thrilled that the girls were getting the recognition they deserved. Martha and Yolanda headed toward the stage, side by side as usual, to a healthy roar of applause.

"But wait!" Mr. Ryan announced from the podium as the girls headed away from the stage after receiving their award. "That's not all!" The microphone squawked with the sound of feedback—so loud and shrill that even Megan reacted. She tugged on her hearing aid and made a sour face. She turned her attention to Jann to find out what Mr. Ryan was talking about.

"This year," Mr. Ryan continued, "I have a special award for one very special exhibit that managed to break through the difficult and often perilous barriers of scientific collaboration." He held up a rather ornate purple ribbon, festooned with a variety of absurd purple gemstones.

Megan and Alexis turned toward each other in disbelief. Their jaws fell slack and their eyes opened wide.

"My fellow scientists and their parents," Mr. Ryan continued, "I'd like to present the first annual *purple* ribbon to Megan Merrill and Alexis Powell for their fourth-grade contribution to the science fair, 'Hamsters Prefer Purple'!"

Megan and Alexis grabbed each other and jumped up and down. Justin jumped up and down as well, even though he didn't understand the happy news.

"Hurry, hurry," said Cindy, tugging on their sweatshirts. "Go get it, girls!"

Megan and Alexis ran for the stage.

13

Positively Purple

"HURRY UP, DADDY," SAID MEGAN. SHE WAS expecting a house full of party guests in less than an hour—and her dad was still screwing in lightbulbs on the front porch. Megan wanted everything stowed away for the party; she didn't want her dad straddling a ladder on the front porch.

"Just finished," said Megan's dad, giving the last lightbulb a twist. He looked down at Megan and said, "Hit the switch."

Megan had scheduled the party so that it began at that purple hour, at about dusk. When she did a test-run on the switch, the front of the house glowed with purple lightbulbs, just like the sky. "Excellent," said Megan. "Even the outside is positively purple."

Matt was in the front hall finishing the last bundle of purple balloons. The archways were decorated in swags of purple crepe-paper streamers. Megan had spruced up the banisters with purple plumes.

"Enough purple," said Matt—between puffs as he inflated what seemed like the bazillionth purple balloon.

"Never enough," said Megan.

"If I blow up one more balloon," said Matt, tying a knot on the last balloon, "I'm going to be purple myself."

Megan laughed.

"I'm serious," said Matt. "This is the last one. I have to get dressed in my uniform and get over to Coach Blazer's house. We're supposed to take the team picture before it gets too dark."

"You're going to miss my party!" Megan protested. "You're going to miss my birthday cake and my birthday candles!"

"Megan, you're throwing a slumber party," said Matt. "It's going to last all night long. I'll be back right after the photo, so don't worry. I won't miss the cake!"

"Promise," said Megan.

"Promise," said Matt.

"You better," Megan warned. "Where's Mom?"

"Making the cake in the kitchen," said Matt.

Megan ran through the den—pausing to arrange the four bottles of purple glitter fingernail polish that were on the table for the special purple manicures the girls would be giving one another later—and into the kitchen to find her mom.

It was Lainee's idea to make a yellow cake with purple frosting. "If the batter were purple," she said, "it might look too dark. Even darker than chocolate. But if we balance the purple frosting with yellow cake, people will be able to see the purple and appreciate the difference."

"Good idea, Mom," said Megan. "But I want purple frosting."

"And you're having purple frosting," said Lainee. "But I'm doing the lettering in yellow so that it stands out."

"But purple candles," said Megan.

"Don't worry. Purple candles," said her mom. She dropped a big glob of purple frosting on the cake and began smoothing the edges with a spatula.

"I want it perfect, Mom," said Megan. "Even if Dad says that perfect isn't a problem in the Merrill family." She was pouring the grape juice and the ginger ale into a punch bowl for the special purple punch.

"When did your father say that?"

"When I was upset with Alexis," said Megan. "Dad said she was probably trying extra hard to be perfect because Justin was maybe not one-hundred-percent perfect. So I asked him if we do that. And he said we don't have any problem not being perfect."

Lainee paused in her cake decoration and held the spatula aloft. "I think what your father was trying to say," she explained, "is that nobody's perfect. We all have our strengths and we all have our limitations."

Megan went to the freezer and pulled out a bunch of ice-cold grapes. She dropped them in the punch bowl as well. "What's a limitation?" she asked.

"Like a weakness," Lainee continued. "We have to learn to accept our strengths *and* our weaknesses—because both of them make us who we are."

"Okay, I get it," said Megan. "Nobody's perfect." She pushed the punch bowl to the middle of the counter so it wouldn't get knocked onto the floor, and she wiped her hands clean on a kitchen towel.

"Yes. For example," her mother continued, "I've been asking you to get that bag of purple feathers out of the dining room for two weeks—"

"Nobody's perfect, Mom!" said Megan.

"Do it," said Lainee.

"I'll do it," said Megan, "if you don't mess up the cake."

Lainee snuck a lick of purple frosting off the end of the spatula and smiled. "I will if you will," she said.

"Deal," said Megan.

Before she left the kitchen, Megan dropped in front of the computer and switched on the Internet connection.

"What are you hopping on the Internet for?" asked her mother.

"I promised Lizzie that I would video instant message her so she could come to my party even though she lives an hour away," said Megan.

"Megan, don't you think that's a bit much?" her mom asked, exasperated.

"Mom, she wants to meet my friends!" argued Megan.

Lainee held up her hands in defeat. "It's your party," she said.

With that matter settled, Megan ran into the dining room. She grabbed the bag of purple feathers off the sideboard and looked for a quick place to stash it before the party. Unfortunately, the drawers of the sideboard were full and the cupboards underneath were packed with platters and dishes.

I don't have time for this, thought Megan.

She darted into the front hall and opened the closet door. It was crammed with overcoats, raincoats, galoshes, and umbrellas.

Megan spotted a tote bag on the floor packed with Matt's baseball equipment. *Perfect*, thought Megan. She stashed the bag of purple feathers in the palm of Matt's baseball glove for safekeeping and tucked the glove back into the tote bag. Then she pushed the closet door shut, grabbed on to the banister, and flung herself upstairs to change for the party.

Since it was a slumber party, Megan had instructed her guests to wear "purple pj's" and to bring a change of clothes for breakfast in the morning. Megan's mom had agreed to make blueberry pancakes for breakfast, but she had said, "Nothing purple after that. All things must end."

Megan had already decided to wear a really dark purple pajama top with a really bright pair of purple pajama pants. The top was decorated with daisies and the bottom was decorated with ducks, but Megan figured that didn't matter. *Purple goes with purple, and the more purple, the better*, she thought. *Besides, it's a little less than perfect and all the better for it.*

She had hardly finished buttoning the top and tugging on her purple fuzzy slippers when the front doorbell began to ring.

It was Kaitlyn, wearing a long lavender night-gown. She waited at the door with an overnight bag over her shoulder and a wild purple birthday present in her hands. "Happy Birthday, Megan," she screamed, beside herself with giggles.

"You're the first one!" cried Megan.

It wasn't long before Casey and Maya joined the party. Casey wore a long plum-colored bathrobe, and Maya had on a long baggy lavender T-shirt. And then three more girls, Tracy, Kim, and Melinda, arrived at the door. Only six girls had arrived so far, but already the decibel level in the house was threatening to go through the roof.

Matt nudged his dad and said, "The nice thing about boys is they're *quiet*!"

Megan's dad said, "I'm with you."

Right on cue, the front doorbell rang and all the girls screamed again. Matt opened the door to find Cindy on the doorstep in an extremely silly pair of violet pj's.

"Am I late? Am I late?" she cried, visibly upset. "I hate being late!"

"You're not late!" snapped Megan, grabbing Cindy's arm and yanking her into the party.

"Oh, no!" cried Matt, looking at his watch. "I'm late too! Mom, where's my baseball uniform?"

"Upstairs," Lainee shouted from the kitchen.

Matt charged upstairs two steps at a time.

Megan and Cindy headed for the living room, where all the other girls burst into shrieks, squeals, and giggles at their arrival.

David winced. "I'm ready when you are," he shouted after Matt, dangling the car keys. "I'll be waiting in the car!"

David opened the door to find two more girls on the doorstep.

"Hello," he said. "What are your names?"

"Elizabeth," "Bethany," the girls murmured politely before bursting into another volley of shrieks at the sight of Megan behind him.

"Is everybody here now?" David asked Megan as the girls pressed past him and into the party.

"Almost, Dad," said Megan.

David tried to exit once more but ended up holding the door for Trina and Keisha, the Dunbar twins, who were running up the walk with big purple birthday presents in their hands.

"Say hello to Lizzie!" Megan cried.

Megan and eleven of her friends crammed into the kitchen alcove to holler "Hey!" into the camera at Lizzie.

On the screen Lizzie was wearing a purple nightcap and purple sunglasses and waving "Hey" right back to them. She blew a noise-maker and tossed a handful of confetti into the air.

Cindy leaned low into the camera frame and signed, "Hey, Lizzie, remember me?"

"Of course, Cindy!" Lizzie signed. She had met Megan and Cindy at the same time at summer camp. "Hey! You guys have to sing 'Happy Birthday' to Megan with me!"

The girls started singing a ragtag version of "Happy Birthday" into the camera, but Megan interrupted. "Wait, you guys, not yet," she protested. "Not everybody is here yet!"

"Who's not here?" asked Lizzie.

At that moment Matt charged downstairs. "Mom, I can't find my baseball glove!" he hollered. "I need my baseball glove for the team photograph!"

"Where'd you leave it?" said Lainee.

"I don't know, but I can't leave home without it!" said Matt, pushing through the girls in his baseball uniform to cross the kitchen.

"Look at Matt in his uniform!" said Tracy, as Matt nudged past. All the girls cooed and chattered excitedly.

Megan leaned toward the computer camera so that she could sign to Lizzie and point across the kitchen at Matt. "Lizzie, that's my brother, Matt, in his new baseball uniform!"

"Mom, make them stop," muttered Matt.

"I'm afraid they have us outnumbered," said Lainee. "Megan, have you seen your brother's baseball glove?"

"In the front hall closet," said Megan.

"*Where* in the front hall closet?" asked Matt, shouting to be heard over the noise.

"Girls, girls!" cried Lainee, clapping her hands for attention. "Too much chaos in the kitchen! Say good-bye to Lizzie! I need you to move this party back to the den."

"Good-bye, Lizzie!" the girls chimed toward the computer.

"Good-bye! Happy birthday!" signed Lizzie.

Megan signed, "Thanks! I'll talk to you later!" to Lizzie. Then she corralled the girls and nudged them toward the kitchen door. "Back to the den!" Megan cried.

"What should we play?" cried Cindy. "Pin the Tail on the Purple Donkey?" All the girls laughed as they pressed through the door into the den.

"Or maybe Duck, Duck, Purple Goose!" shouted Maya, and the girls laughed even harder.

"We can't play anything yet," Megan protested, "because all the girls aren't here yet!"

"Who's not here yet?" asked Casey. "Who could it be?"

At that moment, the front doorbell rang. Cindy tugged on Megan's sleeve. "The doorbell! I hear the doorbell!" she said.

"I'll get it!" Megan cried. She crawled over the Dunbar twins on the sofa and ran for the door, skidding on the front hall tiles in her fuzzy purple slippers. Matt was on his knees inside the front hall closet. "Megan," he said with irritation, "my baseball glove is in the front hall closet—where?"

"Right in front of your nose," said Megan, reaching for the door. When she yanked it open, nobody was there. That was odd. Megan stepped into the doorway and looked left and right.

"*Surprise!*" cried Alexis as she jumped from the bushes.

Megan screamed and laughed. It was Alexis. She entered the front hall and the entire gang of girls jumped with excitement.

At that same moment Matt spotted his baseball glove inside the tote bag in the front hall. He snatched the glove and yanked it from its hiding place. Unfortunately, the bag of purple feathers slipped from where Megan had stowed it and sailed clear up to the ceiling where it snagged on the rafters overhead. Big billowing clouds of purple feathers fell onto the girls in the front hall. Feathers plummeted all around and all the girls screamed. It was a fuzzy blizzard of purple, purple everywhere. A snowstorm of purple.

Some girls started spinning with their arms outstretched as the purple feathers swirled past. A few girls opened their mouths to catch the feathers like snowflakes. Other girls pumped their arms like birds taking flight, to keep the flurry of feathers in the air—and the feathers caught in their hair and covered their shoulders and clung to their clothes.

"Oh, no!" cried Matt. His uniform was covered with purple fuzz. "I'll be the only purple player on the entire baseball team!" All the girls laughed.

"Welcome to my Positively Purple Party!" cried Megan. "The most purple party ever!"

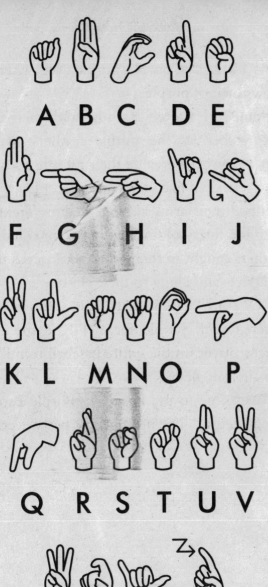

A B C D E

F G H I J

K L M N O P

Q R S T U V

W X Y Z